OUT "A" ORDER

OUT "A" ORDER

EVIE RHODES

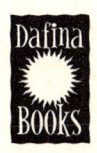

Dafina Books

KENSINGTON PUBLISHING CORP.
http://www.kensingtonbooks.com

DAFINA BOOKS are published by

Kensington Publishing Corp.
850 Third Avenue
New York, NY 10022

Copyright © 2007 by Eva M. Rhodes

All rights reserved. No part of this book may be reproduced in any form or by any means without the prior written consent of the Publisher, excepting brief quotes used in reviews.

All Kensington titles, imprints and distributed lines are available at special quantity discounts for bulk purchases for sales promotion, premiums, fund-raising, educational or institutional use.

Special book excerpts or customized printings can also be created to fit specific needs. For details, write or phone the office of the Kensington Special Sales Manager: Kensington Publishing Corp., 850 Third Avenue, New York, NY 10022. Attn. Special Sales Department. Phone: 1-800-221-2647.

Dafina Books and the Dafina logo Reg. U.S. Pat. & TM Off.

ISBN 0-7582-1666-1

First Kensington Trade Paperback Printing: January 2007
10 9 8 7 6 5 4 3 2 1

Printed in the United States of America

*As always, my book is dedicated to the Lord Jesus Christ!
Thank you, Jesus, for giving your all!*

And

*To my husband, James Rhodes!
Thanks once again for helping
the vision come true!*

Acknowledgments

A most warm and gracious thanks to The Lord Jesus Christ. There's no me without you.

Sincerest and heartfelt, thanks to my husband, James Rhodes. Thank you for being my rock! I love you, love you, love you Jimmy Rhodes, and I want the world to know!

And to all those special people who help me carry the vision—much love to you: Karen Thomas, my very wonderful editor. Thanks for believing in my works. The entire Kensington Publishing family, thank you for what continues to be a great opportunity!

Robert G. (Bob) Diforio, thanks for sharing and nurturing!

To the distributors, wholesalers, jobbers, booksellers, librarians, Book Clubs, radio stations and television affiliates, thanks so much for your support of my works. It means the world to me.

Peggy Hicks, TriCom Publicity you're wonderful. Thank you for believing in me!

Pamela Walker-Williams, you are the master of webmasters! Thank you.

A warm and special thanks to The Oxygen Television Network and Kim Fucillo, for their wonderful advertising planning with my novel *Criss Cross*.

Doug Ingber, Director and Film Editor, Ingber Television, you are simply the best. Jimmy and I love you but you know that! Thanks for visualizing my vision on the highest level.

Patrick Adams, you never fail to amaze me with your gifts and your contribution to my gifts. You are my "Star" Producer! Thanks for the original score on the commercial and film trailer for *Criss Cross*.

And to my readers, you are everything! Thank you for sharing your time when reading my works, writing to me, and sharing the works with others. You're a precious find in my life!

May The Lord Bless You All!

To all who know me, I remain Standing In Da Spirit!

Author's Note

I was born in Newark, New Jersey, and decided to use this city as a base for a story that I felt was very important in its telling. However, I have fictionalized the city, specifically "the Central Ward," to a great degree, in order to create a world all it's own.

I'd like to personally thank the city of Newark, New Jersey, "the Central Ward," and its residents for being the model for the springboard of my imagination.

I wish the city of Newark and its residents every blessing.

Evie Rhodes
P.O. Box 320503
Hartford, CT 06132
evierhodes@evierhodes.com
www.evierhodes.com

MISSING IN ACTION
(M.I.A.)

*I don't shout my lyrics like all the rest,
my name is Prophecy 1, and I'm doing my best,
no hype, no pipe, no gimmicks, see,
no perpetration to sell a million, G.
I ain't down with the blunts, either, you know,
I think a mind is a terrible thing to blow.
I also ain't riding with a gat in my skirt.
To blow a brother away would cause
me deep hurt.*

*Don't want to see another missing
in action G, too many brothers missing
in action see a wars a war it says, yeah
that's me, M.I.A., M.I.A. , M.I.A. on the
Home front see. It's as Out "A" Order
as can be. Another one is claimed by the
streets.*

*I don't own a jeep, or cruise the streets,
it don't mean I ain't down with the
knowledge though see, I'm a rebel with
a cause that's what they say about me, cuz
on the QT, been there you see. I know about
the pain, yeah it knawed at me, I know all
about hypocrites see, I know about rage
turned inside out and I know about not caring,
without a doubt, but still you've got to be careful
you see.*

*Don't want to see another missing
in action G, too many brothers missing
in action see, a wars a war it says, yeah
that's me, M.I.A., M.I.A., M.I.A. on the
Home front see. It's as Out "A" Order
as can be. Another one is claimed by
the streets.*

*Now I'm not going to snow you or
sell you short, I been well learned and
I'm self-taught. It cost a lot to bring the
truth see, to tear down walls of hypocrisy,
to get into the ghetto and save a soul, to
break a strong and demonic hold, to face
down the spirits that have a grip, to stare
a lie in the face and let it rip.*

*Terror in our neighborhoods, sleepless
nights it just ain't no good. Tomorrow's
leaders caught in war in the hood, reigning
terror just cuz you know you could. Mind
games somebody's being played. We're
slaying our own soldiers and the plans not
laid. Pump it up, glorify. If we can't deal
with our problems we reach for the high.
Don't look now but the price is to die, to
kill yourself or another, M.I.A. there goes
another brother.*

*Now the streets are not our only problem,
tell. We're following images, that can take
us to hell. We follow that image, that's a
lie, and feel good, I'm here to tell ya
Satan told us a lie. The biggest misconception
is we think we've arrived, we turned our backs
on the hood and tried to hide. But you could*

never build a strong foundation, unless the
truth of the Gospel, spreads like a street sensation.
So come on open your eyes, let the truth be.

Cuz we're also missing in action, you see.

If we want justice we're gonna have to
make our own. Put our sins aside and atone.
Get serious this ain't no comedy see, step
aside don't play out the image, don't be
hating, be careful see you don't want to
be rated. This ain't the Nielsens this is
real life see, life in the two seven G.
Any change coming down is up to you
and me. Cuz raw and on the line that's the
way I bring it see.

Remember what I said about missing G.
And although I may be a black female,
I've been in the trenches and I've lived
my own hell.

Don't want to see another missing
in action G, too many brothers missing
in action see, a wars a war it says, yeah
that's me, M.I.A., M.I.A., M.I.A. on the
Home front see. It's as Out "A" Order
as can be. Another one is claimed by the
streets.

Another generation comes after you
and me.

Let's live.

Here's some knowledge:

Street wars and spiritual wars are linked.

Evie Rhodes, aka Prophecy 1

Prologue

It was cold. Shivering icy needles jabbed at her body. The needles poked along starting with a slow crawl from the tips of her toes.

The liquid feel of ice water rushed through her veins. It reminded her of the time she was ice-skating and had fallen through the ice, becoming submerged up to her neck. Boy, was she scared! Just as she was now.

There was a dull ringing in her ears. It had squashed out all the other sounds. Maybe that was good because she could no longer hear for the shrieking, screaming confusion that was going on around her.

God, it was so dark. She didn't want to be in this place by herself. Her fingers were going numb. She floated as parts of her system shut down, distancing her from the searing pain that had rammed into her, knocking her to the ground.

A scorching black jabbing pain had shot through her chest cavity, leaving a trail like a blazing forest fire. She grew warmer. She couldn't feel the cold any longer. Up ahead of her was a bright light. She drifted toward the light so she could stay warm. She didn't want to be in the dark alone.

"Daddy!" she called, the sound coming out as though her voice were a whistling teakettle. It was the last time she ever spoke. A whoosh of air exhaled from her damaged lungs, exiting out onto the streets of Newark.

She had a last lucid thought, one that skirted the edges of adulthood although she was a child. *I'm only eight years old. I don't want to die.*

She gave a last hushed breath, barely audible, and all sound and feeling ceased to exist for her.

A moment ago the air had been still, but now the trees rustled with the spirit of the unknown, leaving the dead child as though she were no more than a carcass lying on the street.

Chapter 1

Aisha Jackson ran up to Jasmine. She tagged her. "You're it," she shouted.

Jasmine stomped her foot, starting to count. "Ten, nine, eight, seven, six . . ."

The kids squealed, laughing. They ran to find hiding places. At the corner of the block several young men were hanging out.

Standing on the corner of Muhammad Ali Boulevard and 18th Avenue as though he owned it, and everything within its range, was Temaine Perry, who was seventeen years old.

He was a tall, rangy, wiry youth, with an edgy, moody personality. His dark edge was a source of attraction, but his restlessness was a magnet of trouble.

Never one to miss a shot he said, "Man, Ballistic is trying to roll down on niggas. It's time to drop that nigga. He can't get no action on this turf. That punk is from Irvington. How does he think he's gonna get a slice of Newark's pie? This is Port Newark, baby. We is running things up in here."

Rico DeLeon Hudson was nineteen years old. He was serious, methodical, and as territorial as a panther, roaming the jungle. Although he was a good two inches shorter than Temaine's six feet one inches, there was no doubt he was the leader. He was persona grata—respected, awed, and not to be played with.

Rico had been dodging bullets, running the streets, and true to da game since he was twelve years old. He had also always been the leader.

Everybody who was anybody on the streets knew Rico, who sported a nappy Afro that was always groomed to perfection. His face was angular, sleek, and his eyes emitted one truth, if one looked closely enough. That truth was death. It sprang from the depths of his eyes as lithe as a panther.

His deception was the seeming innocence that oozed from him. He was a mother's nightmare. A slick sheen of charm covered the veneer of who he really was.

Underneath the veneer of innocence was a cold, cruel, calculating mind. He was of a generation that had to have it all, right now, by any means necessary. Coming in second was not an option.

Rico stared at Temaine. They had been running the streets together since elementary school. They had taken a blood oath to always have each other's back. Rico, who was always dressed in the latest sports gear, tugged at the collar of his leather jacket.

He straightened the hood on the jacket and then stuffed his hands in his pockets. He stepped to the curb swearing under his breath.

High up on a roof Spence Parkinson was dressed in black, complete with a black cap pulled low covering his forehead. He aimed the weapon with the scope at Rico. Rico stepped into sharp focus. Spence nodded his head slightly.

Jasmine shouted even louder, "Five, four, three, two . . ." She ran toward the corner. Spence hoisted and balanced the weapon. He zoomed in. The scope teetered back and forth.

Rico stooped down on the side of Temaine. The scope followed him. The red dot centered on his heart. Jasmine careened into Rico, shouting, "One!"

Rico jumped back.

The rifle kicked, and the blast let loose, ripping through the girl-child, Jasmine. Her arms spread like the wings of an angel, her body airborne. The blast lifted her off her feet, knocking her to the ground.

Rico's crew ducked and ran. Kids screamed. A high-pitched wail sliced through air. Rico did not know whose it was, but it shattered him in a deep secret place.

The entire incident had happened in a split second. For an instant every bit of noise on the street became a deafening silence. The kids running up and down froze as though someone had shouted, "Freeze frame."

Rico rolled Jasmine over, staring into the dull expression on the little girl's face. Though it was out of character for him, gently he cradled her in his arms, running a hand through her hair. Blood smeared all over his leather jacket, and the acrid smell of the blood and gunpowder drifted up into his nostrils.

Temaine was bugging. What the hell was Rico doing? He tugged on Rico's jacket. "Let her go, man! Come on! We've got to raise up out of here!"

At the sound of Temaine's voice, Rico recovered, jumping to his feet. They cleared the area as though they had never been in existence. In an instant they were ghost.

A crowd gathered in the street. Jasmine lay faceup on the concrete, where Rico had dropped her. Marcus Simms, who was ten years old and Jasmine's best friend, stared at her lying on the ground.

He trembled as he saw her blood seep into the dirty gutter. He watched it trickle and spill down into the sewer at the edge of the curb.

Her eyes were sightless. Her face was expressionless. She resembled a porcelain doll that had been abandoned in someone's wake. Although the air had been still a moment ago, the trees now shook with an unknown spirit.

Marcus stared into the trees, watching what amounted to a mist until it disappeared. He heard an unearthly shrieking that pierced the core of his being.

Although he couldn't quite make out the words that were

being shrieked it sounded like something scraping across glass. The sound was high-pitched and shattering.

From the corner of his eye he saw a huge pair of black wings flapping, or he thought he did. He blinked. It was gone.

He turned back to the shell that was Jasmine Davenport. Frozen in place, he did not move. Unconsciously he whispered, "Someone please call 911," knowing that in his neighborhood that's all it was, a call, a disembodied voice on a wire. There was no real savior for them on the other end of the line. That thought sent a tear chasing a spot of dirt down Marcus's cheek.

They were standing on shaky ground. That ground was Newark, New Jersey. The Central Ward. Newark's Central Ward was legendary even among the dark and dangerous.

The most curious thing about the Central Ward was the level of cohabitation.

It was home to some of the most notorious, ruthless thugs breathing, as well as to those who were regular citizens struggling for upward mobility.

And of course there was always the low income, those who were simply trapped. Not having any paper to spread around meant they were not captains of their own existence.

They were the forgotten victims sitting on a patch of dirt that society at large had basically given up on, victims of those who knew how to drain money out of misery and were raking in the cream, at the expense of the downtrodden and defenseless.

There were housing apartment complexes that you simply couldn't go in. There were pockets of the Central Ward where death lurked in every corner and crevice. In almost every sound there was the click of a gun barrel, the sliding of a clip or laser rays that tracked human heart beats.

And your own shadow was something you wouldn't see. If you saw a shadow, most likely it would be a silhouette of death.

There were projects where a person could disappear, never to be heard from again. Many a skeleton cried out from behind the cement walls. The projects had their own roaming security—packs of young boys ranging in age from eight to fourteen, had it locked down. Corporate America had never employed security that was as tight as this.

Coexisting right alongside the older apartment complexes were new developments with landscaped lawns, barbecue grills, and bright shiny new Cadillac Escalades in the driveways.

There was a very conflicting contrast between someone trying to make a change, as the new developments were testament to, and those who would not change one iota.

There were those who were as forgotten as the older dilapidated buildings, people leaning out of the windows on hot days, gunshots ringing out from the hallways, or blood flung against the walls.

And even the least of the animals in a jungle knew that it was the fittest of the fit that survived. But these were not animals, these were people. They were living, breathing souls, all trying to survive. In some cases they were trying to survive in surroundings not fit for human habitation and in conditions that should long ago not have existed.

In the final scheme of things the Central Ward was not about surviving. On the surface it appeared to be, but it wasn't. You weren't surviving if you were scared to death, trapped, and couldn't get out. You were just one of the living dead. And in this death there was no light.

The mechanism for survival had died long ago; this was defeat, existing but never living. The Central Ward was actually about law and lawlessness, and what the rulers thereof decided.

On the corners of these streets the churches, the bodegas, the liquor stores competed for passing bodies. Needless to say the churches weren't winning out. And no one could really figure out why.

The churches were dying on the same corners as the people, since there was a lack of youth to fill the inside pews. There were barely any children to add their voices to the choir.

Although the body drops were occurring at an alarming rate, there were no bodies to fill up the pews in search of salvation, freedom, or hope. An entire two generations were missing from the churches.

Business at Perry and Whigham funeral homes, which were located around the corner from each other, was at an all-time high. They were raking in the remains of what the churches did not. Death had become a profitable business in the black community.

Death was the only real means of escape. It was, for some, the only way to get out.

And then there was the darkness—it sprouted from the souls of men, it danced in their blood spilled in the streets, and it permeated the very air they breathed.

They lived with darkness on a daily basis, even when the sun was shining. Yet they didn't see it and couldn't really comprehend it. Darkness had become an invisible shroud.

They didn't know what it truly was. And they didn't know its name. Not really, because they didn't believe in the savior, they didn't believe they could combat the darkness.

They thought that was just the way it was. Deceit was at its highest level, the players being played because they didn't believe they had the power to change it. And if you didn't believe in power you couldn't receive it.

Such was the Central Ward.

The tragedy of it was they didn't see it. Couldn't see it. God, why couldn't they see it? Death was an alternate escape route.

Little Jasmine Davenport had escaped. Marcus Simms, who sat watching her lifeblood disappear into the sewer, had seen but as of yet he didn't know what he'd seen.

"Someone please call 911," he whispered for the second time that day into an empty pit where no one seemed to answer. His voice was a small echo in a really big abyss.

After all, this was the Central Ward. There really wasn't any hurry. Was there?

Jasmine Davenport was only one of the children who were lost. And she could count herself lucky because she had escaped with her soul.

There were many others who would not.

* * *

Welcome to the Central Ward.

And be forewarned, you will need to see with your spirit, not just with your eyes.

Upon this reading you have crossed a realm and entered a different world. It is a world that coexists by its own laws.

And that world is in and of itself OUT "A" ORDER! Believe that.

Chapter 2

Finally there was a rush for the little, dead black girl in the vehicle with the red flashing lights. The ambulance carrying Jasmine screeched to a halt in front of Beth Israel Hospital. The lights flashed. The sirens rang out full blast.

And the equivalent of a black beast passed in their midst, invisibly viewing the spoils of its own revenge. Its latest carcass was little Jasmine Davenport.

The medical attendants jumped out of the back door. They hauled the stretcher holding Jasmine, with breakneck speed, through the emergency room doors. They were a day late and a dollar short, but the appearance of saving a life needed to go on.

Jasmine's daddy, Shannon Davenport, thirty-six years old, a tall, slim man, was right on their heels. Fire, devastation, and despair were competing with each other from under his heavily lashed eyes.

He had insisted they bring his daughter to Beth Israel, although UMDNJ was where she should have gone. In retrospect he would realize this request was nothing more than misplaced pride and authority in a situation in which he'd had absolutely no control.

The medical attendants hauled the stretcher through another set of doors. He did not miss a step. He was right behind them.

A young doctor blocked his path. "I'm sorry, you can't go in there."

He pushed the doctor with brute force. He flew backward, landing on his behind. As Shannon reached down to grab him by his collar, a white police officer in uniform issued a choke hold on him from behind.

He dropped low, elbowing the cop in a soft spot, breaking the hold. The cop landed on the floor with the breath knocked out of him.

The doctor scrambled to his feet, looking a little dazed. A short distance away a black uniformed officer watched the unfolding scene with interest. He saw his partner put his hand on his gun.

Deciding it was definitely time to swing into action, he ran over to where the commotion was taking place. "That's enough. You just hold it right there," he said to Shannon Davenport. He put out a warning hand to keep him in his place while helping his partner to his feet with the other hand.

"Now, just who are you?" he said.

"I'll tell you who he is. He's a stupid punk who's going to jail," the officer who had been knocked to the floor said.

Shannon glared at him. "When hell freezes over."

The doctor, not liking where this was heading, spoke up. "Just a minute. Maybe I can be of some help here. Are you with the little girl who was just brought in?"

"Yeah."

"What's your name?" the doctor said.

"Shannon. Shannon Davenport. That's my little girl in there. I need to know that she's going to be okay."

The police officers relaxed. This man was one of the many distraught parents they ran into when they were working the emergency room shift. Although they did not like his actions, under the circumstances they decided to forgive them for the time being.

The officer who had been knocked to the ground said, "I'm sorry. I didn't know. No harm done. Okay?"

Shannon nodded.

The black officer sighed, rolling his eyes at the ceiling.

"Mr. Davenport, your daughter was radioed in as critical. It only complicates things to have people in the room who are not part of the procedure. Just let us try to stabilize her first. I promise as soon as she is stable I will personally come out and talk to you. Okay?"

He put a soothing hand on Shannon's shoulder. Shannon nodded. His face was etched in grief, a picture of both gut-wrenching hope and the truth hovering behind denial.

"How about a cup of coffee while you wait?" the black officer said.

"Yeah. Okay. Thanks."

Behind the closed doors Jasmine lay in a bed on a mound of white sheets and blankets. Blood was staining the hospital linen at an alarming rate. The atmosphere was tense. They had hooked her up to monitors. Tubes were protruding from her arms and mouth.

A small platoon of doctors diligently worked on her. A number of nurses assisted. They did everything they could to restore life to the little girl's lifeless body, but it was to no avail. Finally they had exhausted every possibility.

The young doctor who Shannon Davenport had knocked to the floor looked at the monitor, seeing the flat line. He ran a hand through his hair.

He bowed his head in despair. "Damn. Not again." He glanced at the small, still face of the little girl. She was a beautiful child who had turned out to be another body drop.

"She's gone. The truth of the matter is she was gone when she got here. But we had to try," an older doctor said.

The doctors and nurses slid off their masks. They removed their bloodstained rubber gloves. Someone turned off the pump and various machines, silencing the low hum that had been emitting throughout the room.

The older doctor, sensing the young doctor's despair, put a hand on his shoulder. The young doctor shrugged it off. "This is the third child in a month."

He walked over and glanced at Jasmine's chart. "From the same neighborhood. *What the hell is going on over there?* What kind of monsters gun down children in broad daylight?"

The older doctor sighed. "Look, Peter, there's nothing we can do except try to save their lives when they arrive."

"Someone needs to do that before they arrive, Dr. Spinelli. Because by the time they arrive, most of the time it's too late."

Chapter 3

Tawney Davenport raced through the emergency room doors. Her hair hung limply in a string of wild-looking curls. Tears streaked her face. Her eyes had a haunting savage look to them. She spotted Shannon drinking a cup of coffee.

The emergency room at Beth Israel Hospital was jam-packed. It was a picture of total chaos. Beth Israel received about eighty thousand annual visits, including approximately twenty-four thousand annual emergency room visits in pediatrics.

This made for a hot bed of emergency medical treatment that was needed at any given time. Located in the heart of Newark, Beth Israel was at its busiest when Tawney ran through its doors.

There were an array of injuries that needed to be attended to, including gunshot wounds, stabbings, domestic abuse, as well as of those who had fallen victim to the savage beast of gangbanging.

Stress was at an all-time high in the neighborhood of Newark, so there were cardiac patients, heart attacks, and a man afflicted with a stroke. High blood pressure was rampant, the silent killer of the black community. It seemed as though the entire city of Newark had turned out for medical treatment.

When Tawney burst through the emergency room doors of Beth Israel, all eyes that could follow her did as she broke through the monotonous wait of pain and suffering.

"Shannon! Oh God, Shannon! Where's my baby? What happened?"

Shannon reached out to gather Tawney in his arms, but she backed away. She knocked the cup of coffee from his hand. Hot coffee splattered all over his shoes.

"Please. Do not touch me. Do not. I want to know what happened to my daughter."

Again he reached for her. Tawney threw both of her hands in the air. She stepped back. "Just tell me this is a mistake. Tell me you didn't let anybody shoot my baby!"

He dropped his head, not meeting her eyes.

"Look at me, Shannon!"

The white police officer moved forward, but his black partner put a restraining hand on his arm.

"Tawney, Jazz is going to be all right. The doctors are going to make sure."

Tawney turned her back. The blood was drumming in her ears. She couldn't believe what he'd said. He must be crazy. She turned back, looking at him as though he were stupid.

She started to speak, sputtered, and then tried again. "The doctors. The doctors are going to make sure my baby is all right. It was your job, Shannon, to make sure my baby was all right."

"The damn doctors are not God! So how would they know? Tell me. How the hell would they know? Hmmm?" Tawney's voice was on high octave, screeching across notes, like that of an opera singer out of control.

Tears shone in Shannon's eyes. His shoulders slumped. He bowed his head. His voice was deep, husky when he spoke. "I'm sorry. She was outside playing with the other kids. The last time I checked she was fine."

At that moment Peter Connelly, the young doctor, stepped through the doors. He walked over to Shannon. He glanced briefly at Tawney. As if on cue, all noises in the emergency room ceased for the briefest of moments.

The silence was absolutely eerie.

"I want to see my daughter, man. Is she all right? My wife and I want to see her right now."

Peter's expression turned solemn. His eyes darted in the cops' direction. Briefly they flitted at Tawney. The cops moved closer.

Peter looked at Shannon. "I'm sorry. We did everything we could. She was too far gone."

Tawney's shrill screams ripped through the air, sending shock waves rippling throughout the room. All motion came to a halt.

"No!" she screamed. "No! Oh God! No! It can't be. My baby is dead. Jazz is dead. I want to see Jazz. Jazz!"

She broke into a run. Everyone ran behind her. She burst through the doors. She saw her daughter lying silently where she had been left. "Jazz. Jazz. Jazz, wake up. It's Mommy. I'm here. Jazz, it's time to wake up now. Come on, Jazz, we have to go home."

Her mind screamed, one long shrieking wail. She couldn't hear herself think. The screaming was too loud. Insanity seized hold of her brain, and for a moment she thought she would faint. But she had to stay on her feet. She had to be there for her baby. She took a deep breath and with it a tentative step toward the remains of her child.

When she reached the bed she looked at the blood-drenched sheets in horror, her face crumbled as though it were only a mask held together by a flimsy foundation. She looked at her little girl's face. Her own became a portrait of wretched, heart-wrenching despair.

She put her face close to Jazz's. She lifted a dead arm to put around her neck. Jazz's arm fell back to the bed. Tawney tried again, this time holding Jazz's arm in place. She put her nose against the child's neck, where a warm pulse should have been beating.

They all looked on. There was nothing to say. Anything said would be the worst type of intrusion. Shannon stood alone with a blank look in his eyes as he watched Tawney holding their dead daughter.

"Jazz, wake up so Mommy can take you home," Tawney whispered to the little girl. At those words Shannon turned away. Pain sliced through him, as though someone had gutted him with a shiv.

The black police officer touched Shannon on the shoulder.

"Mr. Davenport, I'm sorry but we need to ask you a few questions. Would you mind stepping out with us?" Shannon gazed at his wife and daughter, and then shot Dr. Connelly a look.

The doctor lifted his chin for Shannon to go. He moved closer to Tawney, who was still holding and whispering to her daughter.

Another child lost in the belly of the beast.

Chapter 4

The police led Shannon to a small office that was cramped and tight, which they used as a miniheadquarters on the premises of the hospital. There was a single lightbulb, a desk, and a couple of chairs.

It was definitely not the friendliest of environments. It was certainly not an environment for a grieving parent who had lost a child.

"Have a seat, Shannon. I'm Officer Campbell. My partner here is Officer Lombardo," the black police officer said.

Shannon took a seat. Campbell perched on the edge of the desk. He pulled a pad and pen from his pocket. Lombardo chose to stand in the corner.

"I'm sorry to have to put you through this so soon after the shooting of your daughter. But the quicker we move, the better chance we have of catching her killer. Mr. Davenport, do you know who shot your daughter?" Officer Campbell said.

Shannon laughed. "If I knew who shot my daughter, do you think I'd be sitting here?"

Officer Lombardo jumped in. "It's our job to catch the person who shot her, Mr. Davenport. Not yours."

"Naw, my man. It was your job to provide safe streets before this happened. Now she's dead, so that means you don't have a job."

Lombardo leaped from his corner. "Just what the hell does that mean? We do everything we can."

Shannon was on his feet, shaking with rage. "Everything wasn't good enough. Was it, Lombardo? Because if it was, my wife wouldn't be holding a dead child in her arms."

Lombardo was awash with guilt, frustration, and rage. The streets of Newark were a ticking time bomb. He had no desire to carry the full weight of it on his shoulders. Still, the combination of squalor and the cash-rich streets irked him in a place that he'd rather not visit.

New Jersey had a 130-mile coastline and two major seaports, New York/New Jersey and Philadelphia/Camden. Port Newark and the Elizabeth Port Authority Marine Terminal, part of the New York/New Jersey Seaport, together constituted one of the largest containerized port complexes in North America.

As a result the streets of Newark were a cash-rich, criminal enterprise, with an undetermined amount of drug traffic crisscrossing the city. The bottom-line result was that Newark's crime rate was more than two times the national average.

The helplessness of the situation washed over Lombardo. He lashed out at Shannon. "Those are your streets and your neighborhoods. What the hell are you doing about it? I don't see you people doing a damn thing but complaining."

Campbell slid off the desk. He couldn't believe Lombardo had gone there. He had said, "You people." Any fool of a different race knew better than to use that term.

He couldn't believe Lombardo had let his anger get the better of him, although he was known to be a bit touchy, as well as a bit of a hotshot on the streets.

Campbell's face was dark with an unnamed emotion. Lombardo had committed an unpardonable offense. Campbell quickly closed the distance between them. "You're out of line, Officer," he spat at him through clenched teeth.

He stared Lombardo down until he had the decency to look away. Realizing his offense, Lombardo clamped his mouth shut. He yanked the chair from under the desk. He paused with his hand on it.

The tension grew.

A spot of spittle appeared in the corner of Shannon's mouth as he gazed at Lombardo in impotent rage. His fist was clenched rock hard at his side. He was so mad a tremor raced through his body. This bastard had balls, and Shannon was just the one to chop them off for him.

"What's up?" Shannon said in a nasty gutter tone.

Lombardo released the chair. "Whatever you want it to be."

Campbell saw a flash of impending doom. Whether the two of them realized it or not they were both frustrated by the same statistics. But their being on opposite sides of the race card was making this territory shaky ground.

He stepped between the two of them. "Enough."

"Naw. You ain't seen enough yet. But you will." Shannon looked Lombardo up and down. He stormed to the door and threw a last malicious look over his shoulder, before slamming the door shut behind him.

Campbell threw his pad and pen to the floor. He kicked over one of the chairs in frustration. He'd heard about the shooting of the little girl on the police scanner before she'd arrived at Beth Israel Hospital. Her murder was sheer savagery at its worst. Another grandstand play in the Central Ward.

Jasmine Davenport had been a beautiful little black girl with red ribbons all tied in her hair.

Now all that would be seen of her was another hood memorial of balloons, candles, flowers, and ribbons tied on the street corner. The ghetto equivalent for remembering. Another innocent child lost in the jungle.

It felt like these memorials were all over the Central Ward, and he was tired of seeing them. They were enough to make you want to lie down and weep.

They represented loss and despair, but primarily they represented hope lost, life reduced to the ashes of a symbol. It was a constant reminder that they weren't winning the war.

And a war it was, although nobody took responsibility for declaring it. They were fighting an unseen enemy.

It was tragic beyond endurance, and all it did was sow hatred in the hearts of more men, creating a disturbance like the one that had just transpired between Shannon Davenport and Lombardo.

This was a ticking time bomb. Jasmine Davenport's death would prove to be a catalyst to a pot that was already boiling over.

Lombardo stared at the closed door that Shannon Davenport had left behind him, with open hatred beaming from his eyes. This man didn't have any respect for authority, but Lombardo planned to help him learn it before this was all over.

Shannon Davenport was skirting dangerous ground, very, very dangerous. He was skating on thin ice. And Lombardo knew that this ice couldn't take another blow before it began to crack.

Chapter 5

That night a gang of young men gathered in Rico's basement. The room had an air of masculinity about it. The furnishings were bare, but the room contained an awesome stereo system. A big sixty-inch screen TV, a huge pool table along with a club-size pinball machine.

The room was jammed. There was an air of coiled tenseness. All of the young men were strapped. They had the doors covered, as well as the windows. At the slightest movement, they would blow someone away without hesitation.

Two of them were playing pool. One of them in particular stood out. His name was Eight Ball. He had a bald head, two gold earrings, and glasses. Tattoos were visible on his muscular biceps.

His voice was a deep baritone. He sounded like a bass instrument whenever he spoke. He was Rico's right-hand man. They were very close friends.

T-Bone was also a trusted confidant of Rico's. He was a likable kind of guy, built like a linebacker. He leaned forward and took a shot, sending a ball into a side pocket.

In his excitement over the shot, he accidentally kicked over a library bag with books in it. Some of the books spilled onto the floor.

Eight Ball sighed. "Yo, man, pick up the books."

T-Bone laughed while picking them up. "Chill, man. They ain't gold."

Eight Ball gave him a strange look. "What's considered gold is different for every man, son."

"That might be. But I'd prefer to see mine in gold bars."

Laughter erupted.

There was a slight knock on the basement door. It was opened by a crew member to admit a short pretty young woman named Kesha. She was Rico's lady. She came in carrying a chubby baby girl who was fifteen months old, named Ebony.

Kesha scanned the room. The vibes made the hair on her arms bristle. She wasn't big on Rico's lifestyle. She was actually a nineteen-year-old straight-A student at Rutgers University, majoring in business.

However, she loved roughneck thugs, and Rico fit the bill hands down. He'd talked his way into her pants and she'd gotten pregnant, so here she was.

She knew he was a gangster, but she tried to turn a deaf ear and a blind eye while walking a thin line between both worlds. In the process she reaped the benefits of his ability to generate major paper.

The truth be told, this was part of what had seduced her in the first place.

She was a bright girl intellectually, but she liked to show off for her girlfriends. Rico kept her pockets stuffed with cash, bought her a Jeep to cruise in, and had her hair freshly styled in the top salons every week. She also received the latest in spa manicures and pedicures. So homegirl was sprung.

She had it like that, and liked to flaunt it to all her friends. She knew they were jealous because she had snagged this ghetto player, and she liked to keep it like that. She wanted to be top dog and untouchable among them.

The present atmosphere that was making the hair stand up on her arms was just part of the payment. She figured when she graduated from the university with her degree she'd get out and her real life could begin.

A nigga couldn't holla at her because he had paper, then because she'd be generating her own paper, and with her talent for business economics she'd be gracing the front pages of *Business Week* and *Black Enterprise* magazines and others like them in about six years.

She walked up to Rico, managing a smile. "Ebony wanted to say good night to her daddy."

Rico chucked the little girl under her chin. He cooed at her.

"Dadda," Ebony said. He took the baby girl in his arms. He held her high in the air, which she loved, so she kicked and squealed. Finally, he planted a kiss on one chubby cheek, then handed her back to her mother.

"I'll be up soon, Key. Okay?" he said, using his nickname for her. He was the only person who called her Key and he knew it always softened her up. Rico knew she was disturbed by the heavy gang presence in and around the house, as well as the presence covering the street, but it was necessary.

Kesha nodded and headed back the way she had come. Rico watched her walk away.

Ebony smiled. She reached out a hand for him. As soon as the door closed behind them Rico dropped the mask and paced the room agitatedly. He watched the pool game, not really seeing it, between Eight Ball and T-Bone.

Temaine slouched back in a chair with a moody expression on his face. His long legs were stretched out in front of him. He sucked sullenly on his ever-present piece of licorice.

A telephone rang. Rico reached into his pocket, placing the phone to his ear. "Yeah?" he said.

Dickie's voice floated over the wire. He too was a trusted member of Rico's crew. In their world he was called Eyes and Ears. His job was similar to that of a newscaster. He gathered the facts. He reported, pure and simple.

His profile was low, and no one knew who Eyes and Ears was accept a chosen few. In the present climate of the Central Ward the only person who knew who Dickie was was Rico.

The created distance insured his life span. The information insured his cash flow.

"Word's in my, man. The little sister's lights are out. She's dead."

Rico continued pacing. He stopped in front of Eight Ball. Eight Ball stared at Rico intently. His eyes flashed behind his glasses. He leaned his pool stick on the table.

"And?" Rico said into the phone.

"Ballistic has decided to draw first blood. Yours, man. He hired an independent. Spence Parkinson. He's our triggerman. Mr. Rooftop himself."

A cold smile crept across Rico's face. He clicked off. Eight Ball stood ready.

Rico stared deep into Eight Ball's eyes. "Spence Parkinson is the hit man. He missed. The accident is going to cost him, man, 'cause we don't be hitting no kids. It's a violation of the most sacred street law."

Rico picked up a pool stick. He broke it over his knee.

"For starters I want Spence *dead!* This is my turf, man. I created the ground these niggas are standing on. I'm getting serious paid. I'm the only bankroller on these streets, dawg. Ballistic can't have it. All he's going to get is air shipment in a body bag to his mama's house in Irvington. Understand?"

Rico paced the room again. "Damn. I watched that little girl grow up. We'll be at the funeral at a distance. Leak the word on the street. Spence will take another shot. When he does you'll take him out. You're gonna have to get off the streets after the hit."

Eight Ball nodded.

"Spence is just a weak-ass punk. Ballistic will get my message," Rico continued. "I'll take care of Ballistic in my own time. You can consider that nigga history walking for now. In a New York minute I'm gonna erase that history, and he's gonna see death. Word."

"Where you want Spence buried?" Eight Ball asked.

"Right beside the Davenport girl." Rico looked at Temaine.

"My nigga." Temaine smiled.

Chapter 6

At Jasmine Davenport's funeral a grief-stricken neighborhood of family and friends gathered at the girl's grave site.

It was such a shame.

Jasmine had been a precocious, smart, and loving little girl. She was a giver and had shared with all her friends, even those less fortunate than her.

She'd been like a ray of sunshine in the neighborhood that all of the other children had orbited around. She always hugged and greeted her friends when she came outside to play. She generated warmth and caring that wasn't always common, even among children.

The adults loved her. She could read at levels way beyond her years. This fact alone made her a teacher's favorite. She had excellent manners and she was polite. She'd never been known to be a fresh kid.

Sometimes she ran errands to the corner store for some of the older residents. She'd even pick up their newspapers from their yards or porches and bring them inside for them.

Her death was tragic beyond belief.

Marcus was still frightened at the way she had been killed. He looked shell-shocked. He stood near Shannon and Tawney whom he had practically attached himself to since Jazz's death.

He had begged his mom to let him attend the services. He hadn't wanted Jazz to feel alone as though her friends had abandoned her. It was bad enough she was alone in that big old box. After much drama he had convinced his mother he could handle this, and handle it he would. He stood a little taller trying to rep for his best friend lying silently in her coffin.

Aisha, who was like the other half of Jasmine's tag team, held tightly to her mother's hand. Like Marcus, she had insisted she be in attendance. Under the circumstances they were both displaying remarkable maturity for their ages.

Marcus and Aisha exchanged looks. That one look between them said it all. They were there for their friend Jazz until the end.

Marcus looked up at Shannon, who was tense and withdrawn. His look drew Shannon's attention. Shannon reached for his hand, clasping it warmly in his own.

Rico and his crew were in attendance.

The minister's voice droned on.

A small coffin sat in a circle draped with flowers. Inside, one tiny child rested alone in darkness. All sound and life had ceased to exist for her.

The minister was saying, "Ashes to ashes and dust to dust."

Dressed down in a sharp-looking black suit, Spence cruised up behind some tombstones. He raised his rifle with the scope once again.

This time he would take Rico out.

Spence centered Rico in the hairs of his scope. He had the shot. He took it. Automatic gunfire split the air. Spence tumbled backward. Rico and his crew were armed and ready. Their guns clicked quickly into place. The mourners ran and screamed.

Tawney fell across the top of her daughter's coffin. Shannon looked wildly around trying to spot the gunmen. Shots were still being fired. He threw Marcus to the ground and pulled Tawney off the coffin, throwing his body on top of her.

When the shooting stopped, Shannon looked up to see Eight

Ball standing in front of him with the body of Spence, dripping with blood. There was a gaping hole in the middle of his forehead.

Eight Ball dropped the body into the fresh grave that had been dug for Jasmine. He stood staring at Shannon. Just as quickly as Eight Ball appeared, he was ghost, he disappeared, leaving a stunned Shannon on his knees beside his daughter's coffin.

Cars and Jeeps revved up, rolling out of the cemetery. Temaine shouted out of the car at Shannon, "We take care of our own, Mr. Davenport!" The car careened away, spraying dirt and gravel in its wake.

That night Tawney sat in the corner of her bedroom with her knees pulled up to her chin. The bedroom was decorated with warm muted colors, but she drew no comfort from a room she had once taken great pride in. Her eyes were blank and slightly unfocused.

Shannon got up from the bed. He wandered to the window. He lit a cigarette. "Tawney, we need to talk."

Tawney shot him a cold stare. "About?"

"About? How can you ask me that? Damn it, Tawney, this is not my fault. Jasmine was my daughter too."

Tawney jumped to her feet. "And you think the way to vindicate her death is to resort to your old ways?"

She snapped her fingers. "Just like that, justice is served."

Shannon narrowed his eyes. His voice was dangerously low. "What are you talking about, Tawney?"

"I'm talking about that disgusting little play of power that was acted out at my daughter's funeral. It's not bad enough that I lost my baby, is it, Shannon? Nope. That's not the hell enough. I also have to be subjected to a bunch of petty-ass street gangsters who think that they are the law."

"Let me tell you something. That's why I work every day, because I want to get out. I thought you did too. But I was wrong, wasn't I? Tell me I'm not wrong, damn you."

Shannon said nothing.

"Are you listening to me? People are afraid to go out after dark. Old people are scared to go to the store. In downtown Newark you can be shot just for being down there too late."

"You think I enjoy driving past corners, when I come home at night, filled with angry young black men who would just as soon hurt me, shoot me, and rob me as look at me? No. I'll tell you, I don't enjoy that at all. That's why I was trying to get out. But you don't care. Do you? This is your stomping ground. You've been lying to me. You don't care about getting out."

Tawney panted. She was in deep.

She shook her head. "You're afraid of the real world, Shannon. Why don't you just admit it? But you know what? You can just stay in this hellhole with them and think about how they cost you your daughter."

Shannon nodded at her logic. "This is my world, Tawney. And nobody is going to run me out of it. As for your world, it's a fantasy. All in your head." He pointed to his temple.

Tawney fumed. "Do you want to know what your world is?"

"What? Go ahead. I know you're going to run it down for me anyway, right?"

"Damn straight I am. Try destruction. It is nothing but pure destruction. Satan can't cast out Satan, Shannon."

"Shove it, Tawney." The hint of a smile tugged at Shannon's lips. "You think I miss the streets so much that I would disrespect my dead child's funeral?"

"I think you miss whatever power you perceived yourself as having. I know you hate the fact that I make money and you don't. Maybe you should get a job to keep you busy."

Deadly fury spewed from the depths of Shannon's eyes. Unfortunately, Tawney missed the subtle change.

"Once a gangster, always a gangster. People warned me but I didn't listen. Now you have cost me the only good thing that ever came out of you. And you know what? I hate you for that. Yeah. Uh-huh. I hate your damn guts. I can't stomach the sight of you."

"I'm only going to say this once. So listen closely. I don't know what happened at the cemetery today, but I intend to find out."

His eyes found hers. They gripped her in their malice.

"Yeah. You just do that. You be the law, right?"

Shannon knocked the television from its stand; it banged into the wall with a loud crash. Tawney flinched.

"Naw. I ain't the law. That corporation you work for is the law. It's your law. That's why you didn't have enough time to spend with your daughter. That's why I took care of her. And that's why she's dead now."

He grabbed the DVD player, hurling it out the window. The splintering glass fractured Tawney's nerves.

"You see, Tawney, you've got your priorities backward. You don't need a man. What you need is a toy, li'l girl. One you can play with when you ain't up in that sorry-ass bank you work for. You know, the one that you worship on a daily basis. Your god!"

Shannon swept his arm across the wall unit, knocking all the contents to the floor. She jumped.

"That's your god, Tawney. Instead of saying please, Jesus, why don't you just say please, Mr. Bank? That's your god. So why don't you call on them and see if they can serve you up some justice by bringing your daughter back? They're powerful, right? So let them raise her from the dead. Damn you! Maybe they can write a check and negotiate to get her life back."

Tawney was so wounded and stunned she couldn't utter a word in defense. Guilt raced through her veins at his words. He grabbed her by the shoulders. He shook her so hard her teeth clattered. "Go ahead. Call them, Tawney."

Automatic gunfire shattered the windows. Shannon threw her to the floor. For the second time that day he threw his body on top of hers.

The room erupted in a blaze of gunfire. Holes quickly appeared in the walls, as glass rained down through the room. Then there was silence.

Chapter 7

Downtown Newark was a busy place, even at night. The peddlers, were roaming the streets hawking their wares. There were a lot of people on the streets.

A group of young men were loitering outside the game room as the police cruiser glided leisurely by. Lombardo was at the wheel. Campbell was riding shotgun.

They waved at their fellow officers who were manning the makeshift police station that had been set up at the corner of Broad and Market.

The radio inside the cruiser crackled. "Campbell and Lombardo, you there?"

Campbell reached for the instrument. "We're here. What've you got?"

"What's your location?"

"Broad and Market."

"Good. Get over to Muhammad Ali Boulevard. Reports of automatic gunfire have been reported. And Campbell brace yourself."

"Why?"

"It's the Davenport residence."

Campbell and Lombardo exchanged swift glances as Lombardo jerked the wheel, doing a U-turn in the middle of the street. "Thanks, David. I owe you."

"Not a thing, my man." The dispatcher clicked off. Campbell replaced the instrument in its holder. He and the dispatcher had talked about this case earlier. He had had a feeling it wasn't over. Somehow he'd known it was an open-ended chapter. The girl's father was not going to take this lying down.

He stared thoughtfully out the window.

"What's going on here, Lombardo? The girl gets shot and her distraught father is running behind the stretcher at the hospital. Conveniently a body is dropped into the grave that belongs to the little girl at the funeral. And now automatic gunfire is ripping through my man's house. Is he really a victim? Or is there a bigger picture going on here?"

Lombardo shrugged. "I ran a sheet on him out of curiosity. He hasn't been involved in anything that I can see since the birth of his daughter. All activity on him stopped practically on the day she was born. Unless he's gotten a lot more clever."

Campbell stroked his mustache while staring out of the window. "His daughter was eight, right?"

"Bingo."

"I don't know. If it's just circumstances, then this brother is getting a bad break. If it's more than that, then something is brewing right under our noses. Whatever answer happens to be the right one, one thing is for sure."

Lombardo hooked a corner on two wheels. When the car was back on four wheels it bucked forward.

"What's that?"

"Our Mr. Davenport is one dangerous man. He's not to be taken lightly."

"You ran a sheet on him?"

Campbell laughed. "You might say that. I looked into a different type of law. I discovered an ocean of blood. None with his name attached, but there just the same."

Lombardo tossed Campbell a brief look.

Campbell nodded.

"Well, let's see what my man has to say. But I guarantee you it probably won't be much. We don't have a lot to go on. We might walk out with a big zero, but we're going to have to lean on him heavy tonight."

Lombardo smiled. His voice took on a deadly tone. "Let's do it. If he spills any blood that I can prove in my territory, then I will become his looking glass. There's only one law, and he's not it."

Lombardo put the pedal to the metal, in pursuit of Shannon Davenport.

The street in front of the Davenport residence was filled with people. Police cruisers were in the middle of the street with their flashing lights. Some of the residents were in their nightclothes. Police dogs were roaming the street sniffing for a scent.

The car carrying Lombardo and Campbell squealed to a halt. They jumped out. Rushing through the crowd, they made their way up onto the porch.

The living room was decorated in soft leathers with a touch of class. A scattering of sofas sat throughout the room. A beautiful large aquarium took up almost an entire wall in the room.

Exotic fish in a beautiful array of colors swam nonchalantly through the water. There was also a gold birdcage hanging from the ceiling that was empty.

Tawney was standing in a corner with a blanket wrapped around her shoulders. Her hands were wrapped around a mug of hot chocolate as though her life depended on it.

Shannon was smoking and looking out of a side window with his back turned to the entire chaotic scene. A brightly colored parrot sat on his shoulder.

The police were roaming around with gloves on and little plastic bags in their hands. Campbell and Lombardo strolled into the living room as though they owned the place. They immediately focused on Shannon.

"Trouble again, Mr. Davenport?" Lombardo said.

Shannon stubbed out the cigarette in a nearby ashtray. He never turned from the window. "Back off, cracker."

Lombardo's face turned a bright shade of red. "We can do this nice, Davenport, or we can do this different. It's your choice."

"We can do this any way you want, Mr. Police Officer. It don't make a damn bit of difference to me." He turned away from the window to face Lombardo.

Campbell stepped forward quickly. "We'd like to do this orderly."

Shannon exploded. "Orderly. You want to do this orderly?"

The parrot flew off his shoulder to the top of his cage.

"You call this order? This is definitely out a' order, my man. A bunch of street punks shoot my daughter. Then they arrive at her funeral and do another body drop, and tonight automatic gunfire rips through my bedroom where I sleep with my wife, and my daughter isn't cold in her grave yet!"

Shannon's eyes shot flames of fire. "And you! You! Instead of being out on the streets you're in my house, in my damn house wanting to question me again. Right? Well? Isn't that right?"

The police didn't answer.

"And you want to talk to me about order. I don't think so. I'll tell you what I think. This is *out a' order!* This is *out a' line!* This is all a lie!"

Shannon pointed to his wife. "She's living a lie."

Lombardo and Campbell looked at each other. Tawney never came out of her stupor. Shannon pointed at Lombardo and Campbell. "You're living a lie."

He pointed to the rest of the police. "They're living a lie. This whole damn world is living a lie. But you want to know something?"

He walked directly up to Campbell eyeball to eyeball. "I'm a man who knows how to get to the bottom of lies. Believe that. Now, if you still want to talk to me you can do it downtown, because as you can see, my wife is in no condition to listen to this."

Campbell nodded. He turned to Lombardo. "We'll wait for him outside."

Lombardo seethed. Smoke could've popped out of his ears. He clapped his hands. "Nice performance, Davenport. Certainly Oscar-worthy."

Shannon lunged for him. The cops positioned themselves.

Campbell stepped firmly in front of him. "It's not worth it.

You'll lose," he whispered so only Shannon could hear. Shannon took a deep breath. Lombardo put his hand on his nightstick.

Campbell pointed to the street. "That's us. You've got three minutes."

Shannon put his mouth close to Campbell's ear in turn. "Yeah. Okay. But you'd better teach that dog some new tricks, because he's out of bounds."

Campbell observed the pulse that was beating heartily in Shannon's neck. He nodded to appease him and calm the waters.

Shannon walked into the kitchen.

The parrot flew off the top of his birdcage, landing on Shannon's shoulder.

Tawney's mother was sitting at the kitchen table. She had a scared look on her face. The day had gone from black to blacker to midnight. And right now she felt like they were all treading fires in the midst of hell. She was casting nervous glances into the living room.

And meanwhile all she could see in her mind's eye was her granddaughter picking flowers from among the weeds to give to the old people, so as to brighten their day.

Once she had asked her why she did it. Jasmine had treated her to a beautiful look of innocence. "Because it makes them smile, Grandme," she said, using the nickname she had created especially for her grandmother.

"Mama Sue, can you stay with Tawney?" Shannon said, breaking into her memories.

He already knew Tawney's mother would not be leaving his house unless it was under gunpoint. She wasn't about to leave her daughter in the midst of this madness.

It was a strictly mechanical question on his part. He needed something to say. He had always respected Tawney's mother because she knew how to mind her own business. She also knew how to have a person's back.

She gave him a shrewd look. "Where are you going?"

"Downtown with the police."

"Why?"

"Because the police are fools who don't know where to search for real clues. And because I have a criminal record."

"You haven't been in any trouble since Jazz was born, Shannon. Surely they don't think . . ."

He touched her gently on the shoulder. "My own woman isn't sure. How can I expect them to be?"

Tears glistened in Mama Sue's eyes. Shannon was like a son to her. She had always believed in him. Even when he was in the streets, there was a trait to him that was somehow different.

She didn't let him down now. "Well, I'm sure, Shannon! You wouldn't have anything to do with this and I know it. Nobody's going to tell me any different."

Tears glistened in her eyes at the losses and the heavy cost they were all paying.

Shannon dropped a light kiss on her temple. "Thanks. I always said you were worth your weight in gold. I was right."

"Be careful, baby," Mama Sue said, reaching for his hand.

"Don't worry. Just take care of Tawney for me. Okay? She isn't taking this too well. Justice is right around the corner."

He strode out of the kitchen. Mama Sue watched him with a troubled expression on her face.

As Shannon reentered the living room the parrot flew off his shoulder back to the top of its gilded cage. "Ark. The police are fools. The police are fools. Ark. The police are fools," he mimicked Shannon.

The cops turned to stare at the parrot. Shannon smiled. He had trained Pete well. He strode out the front door into the waiting cruiser. The sirens wailed as they sped away into the night. It was just another night in the Central Ward.

Chapter 8

At a deserted warehouse in the Ironbound section of Newark, four young men stood outside a steel door. All of them were underlings, reporting to Ballistic. Unlike so many of the other gangs in the area, they didn't have a name or a moniker.

The only thing close to a moniker that their activities resided under was Ballistic. It was enough to inspire fear, even in those who claimed otherwise.

Ballistic was the grungiest of Newark's crime lords. In the truest of traditions, he was a combination of street thug, old-school Mafia, and the new-millennium criminal enterprise entrepreneurs rising in Newark.

He was one of the savviest, and hands down the most dangerous thug to ever grace Newark's streets.

Ballistic was the Central Ward. He was spawned from its loins although he'd come from Irvington. He was a product of what the Central Ward represented in every aspect of the word. The two couldn't be separated. The Central Ward was targeted, spirited ground. And Ballistic was at the other end of its umbilical cord.

Born in Newark, raised in Irvington, he had moved on to the Newark turf with a simple plan. One was to take over. Two was to turn anybody who got in his way into a corpse. Plain and simple.

He wasn't taking no shorts.

Trey, a sullen-looking young man of seventeen, sauntered up to the small crowd. Neither one of these boys nor the ones in Rico's group was older than nineteen.

"What's up?" Trey said.

Bobby removed the hood of his sweatshirt. His eyes bored into Trey. They shook hands. "You black. You and my man Ballistic." He nodded toward the warehouse.

Warren P. stepped up to Trey. "What's up, money grip? You be summoned by the man too, I see."

Trey nodded briefly. "What's the level on this scene?"

"Spence caught a bad hit. Got body-dropped into the Davenport girl's spot in the ground. The heat is on."

"Where was his cover? I heard about the accident with the li'l girl. Not good." Trey lit a blunt. He blew smoke rings in the air.

Warren P. laughed sarcastically. "Wasn't no cover, Trey. Nigga went buck wild crazy and decided to do a solo. Ballistic don't accept no misses. My man Rico had his ground covered."

At that moment a discreet-sounding buzzer went off. The young men entered the warehouse. Trey put out the blunt with the toe of his boot.

They all filed quietly down a long dark corridor until they reached an open space in the warehouse. There was one chair in the room with the back turned, among a scattering of crates.

A huge muscle-bound German shepherd sat with danger generating from his eyes. He sat at attention watching the men enter.

The room was dark and dank with a single bulb hanging from a suspended wire in the ceiling. They stood at attention until the figure in the chair turned to face them. When he did he stared coldly, while lovingly stroking the dog's head.

Ballistic had a hole in his throat with a breathing tube attached to it. His voice when he spoke was deep and raspy. His eyes sparkled like dark black diamond chips.

He was holding a black cane with a wood handle. He surveyed each of the young men standing before him individually, coldly.

"You niggas think that I am somebody to be toyed with?"

There was a collective shaking of heads as they shifted uneasily in their spots. They knew better than to speak.

"Someone is trying to make a fool of me?"

Complete silence from the crew.

He rose from his seat but not before kissing the top of the dog's head. He rubbed the dog's nose. He walked the room with a noticeable limp. He was dependent on the cane.

The dog sat stock-still. Only his eyes moved while following Ballistic.

"I am not happy with Rico DeLeon Hudson's message to me. Understood? The income from that turf he cannot keep. Because I am king of this patch of land. No?"

He walked up to where he could smell the breath of the first boy he approached. He looked so deeply into the boy's eyes that he could see the blackness of his soul. He continued this ritual until he reached the fifth boy in line.

As he stepped back without warning, his cane whipped through the air. The sharp point of it landed in the heart of the fifth boy. The boy dropped dead without so much as a sound to the concrete floor.

Bobby, Warren P., and Trey stared straight ahead as well as the fourth man in line. Ballistic snorted. He pulled a handkerchief from his pocket.

He blew his nose, sticking the handkerchief back in his pocket. Then he limped his way down the line, back the way he had come.

He halted in front of Trey.

"I want a fear deeper than the depths of hell to fall on Rico in under twenty-four hours." He raised an eyebrow at Trey. Trey stared at him with deadpan eyes. He gave a slight nod.

Ballistic twirled the cane. Trey didn't flinch. He spat a wad of phlegm at Warren P.'s feet. A gurgling sound emitted from the tube in his throat. Warren P. didn't appear to have noticed. Ballistic's gaze found the fourth man. "Clean it up."

The fourth young man stepped past him to do so. Ballistic grunted in disgust. He shook his head before putting his Glock to the base of the young man's head. Then he fired. The body dropped at Warren P.'s feet.

"Five is too many. All I need is three. Trey, Warren, and Bobby. Understood?"

He turned on his cane, limping from the room. The dog gave them a brief look, before trotting behind his master out of the room.

You are listening, aren't you? You should begin to listen with your inner audio as well as your outer audio. You will need more than just your ears to hear.

We're no longer in your world. We're in the Central Ward. And the Central Ward is in and of itself Out A' Order.

Chapter 9

Lombardo glared through the one-sided mirror, with a look of disgust on his face. He didn't know why Campbell insisted on treating Shannon Davenport with kid gloves.

He watched Shannon and Campbell spar off across the table from each other in the interrogation room.

"I can't help you if you won't talk to me," Campbell said.

"You can't help me if I do talk to you," Shannon shot back.

"Who shot your daughter, Shannon? May I call you Shannon?"

"Whatever."

Campbell sighed. He rolled his eyes at the ceiling. "Shannon, who shot your daughter?"

"I don't know."

"Who shot the boy at your daughter's funeral?"

"I don't know."

"Can you describe him?"

"No."

Campbell stood up. He leaned across the table in Shannon's face. "I have eyewitnesses who say he stood as close to you as I am right now. And you don't know what he looks like?"

"No."

Campbell changed tactics. He sat back down. In a friendlier tone he asked, "Who shot up your bedroom tonight?"

"I don't know."

"Any idea why someone would feel the need to plaster your bedroom with bullet holes?"

Shannon shifted uneasily in his chair. Lombardo listened intently on the other side of the glass. Shannon tossed a hostile look at the mirror on his side of the room.

"Maybe they don't like my decorating. Actually, I was hoping you might tell me that. You're the investigating officer."

Campbell got to his feet. He paced the room. "I'm growing weary of playing these word games with ya, black. Just so ya know."

Shannon warmed to the sound of the street code. Finally this cop was speaking his language. "Now we're on the same page, my brother. 'Cause I'm getting sick of you and Rambo pissing off in the wrong direction."

There was a discreet knock at the door.

Campbell opened it. He stepped into the hall. A policewoman handed Campbell a sheet of paper. "There's no sheet on the wife. She's clean. She's a very hardworking young lady. Holds down a respectable managerial position in the bank. Appears to have married wrong, though. I guess you already know the husband has a different story."

"Yeah. It's pretty much what I expected. But I can't afford to leave any rocks unturned. Know what I mean?"

The policewoman nodded. Lombardo appeared. He was itching to get in Shannon's face. "Let me take a shot at him, Campbell."

Campbell and Lombardo entered the interrogation room together. "I have a couple of questions for you," Lombardo said.

Shannon stood up. "I ain't got no answers for you."

Lombardo ignored him. "You have plenty of quirky little incidents that I could drive a tractor trailer through. For instance, why would someone shoot at you after your little girl's funeral?"

Lombardo paused, then continued. "And why would Spence Parkinson's body be dropped into Jasmine's grave?" Lombardo shrugged. "Like maybe Spence killed Jasmine. Revenge or a deal gone bad."

Shannon refused to utter a word. Lombardo moved closer to Shannon. "And maybe you hired my boy at the cemetery to kill Spence. A little revenge of your own?"

Shannon's eyes shot sparks. "Are you charging me with something?"

"No."

"Do you have a reason to hold me?"

"Not yet."

Shannon smiled. "You want me, hunter?"

Lombardo shrugged. "Not unless you step out of line."

Shannon walked to the door. "You don't draw my lines, Little Italy, I do. You're barking up the wrong tree, hunter. You should be out beating the bushes. Any young rookie knows that."

It was Lombardo's turn to smile. "Don't let it worry you. I'm there too."

"Well, make sure you don't step up behind the wrong bush," Shannon issued him a veiled threat.

Campbell stepped in. "You've got eight untraceable years, supposedly clean, Shannon. My advice to you is to keep it that way."

"When I want your advice I'll be sure to run right down to get it, my man. Count on it." Shannon stepped through the door, closing it behind him.

"Any word on the street?" Campbell said to Lombardo.

"Not yet."

"I want to know who killed Jasmine Davenport and why."

"Yeah. It's going to be a sad day if we find her father on the other side of the trigger."

"I guess we better start beating the rookie bushes," Campbell said. "You never know what you might shake out of one."

They both grinned.

Chapter 10

Tawney sat behind her desk in the bank staring at the untouched game of solitaire. Her fingers played out a rhythmic tap dance against her mouse. Her concentration was nonexistent, a thing of the past.

Her office was full of assorted flowers from her colleagues as well as her staff showing their sympathy. Just looking at them made her want to throw up. She practically gagged at the smell of them.

But it would be rude to just throw them in the trash, which is what she felt like doing, while screaming at the top of her lungs. She had never been this edgy in her life.

The loss of her daughter made her feel as though she were walking around in a nightmare. Waves of blackness covered her skin like a veil.

It was hard to believe she would never hold Jazz again in her arms. Or nuzzle the warm spot in her neck. Or watch her run down the street. She wished she hadn't gone there with that thought because it conjured up images of her child being gunned down like a dog in the street.

Whatever.

It was just inconceivable that Jazz was gone. Wrenched from her grasp, while she had been sitting in some damn office, having a normal day. Probably in some mundane meeting, while the life was being snuffed out of her child. It was a complete travesty.

There was a light tap on her office door. She looked up to see Shonda Hunt, who was a member of her staff. Shonda looked at her timidly, "I'm really sorry to disturb you, Tawney. I just wanted . . ."

Tawney waved her into the office. She was trying hard not to be the witch on wheels she was feeling like. She really wanted to tell Shonda to get the hell away from her door.

But that was just not appropriate. Instead she said, "Come on in, Shonda," her voice relaying a calm politeness she did not feel.

Shonda perched on the edge of the chair in front of Tawney's desk. She cleared her throat. "I just wanted to say I'm sorry for your loss. If there's anything I can do . . ."

"No. There's nothing. Thank you for offering."

Gazing at Tawney, Shonda wondered what the hell Shannon Davenport saw in this cardboard, wannabe fashion statement. So she was player hating. So what? She had met Shannon Davenport at last year's office party and she couldn't help but wonder. He was fine as wine.

Tawney's skin, while a carmel brown, was surrounded by a halo of blond hair that flowed past her shoulders. Cat-green eyes completed the picture in a face accented with high cheekbones, indicating a possible Indian heritage somewhere in her genes.

Shonda wanted to throw something at this Oreo cookie, which was all black on the outside and white on the inside. Tawney was tall and slim with a shapely build. She gave off a picture of flawlessness.

Shonda knew better.

Tawney was in fact smooth, intellectual, and corporate with the hots for gangster-type men. Her image was a facade for corporate America, so she could get paid, but it didn't fool Shonda one bit.

Shonda would bet her bottom dollar that Tawney's IQ test—and she was rumored to have an IQ that was extraordinary—hadn't revealed her penchant for slumming in the hood.

After an awkward moment Shonda said, "I know this probably isn't a good time, but I wanted to talk about the written warning in my file. It's just that my performance review is coming up and—"

"Shonda, I'm here, but I'm not really here, if you know what I mean. As soon as I'm able to deal with this I will. Okay? You have my word."

Shonda nodded. "Thanks, Tawney. I'm sorry. I know it's not a good time."

Tawney rose from her desk, stifling the urge to physically throw Shonda from her office. "No, it isn't a good time, but it's not your fault."

Bright tears shimmered in Shonda's eyes, making Tawney feel guilty for thinking about physically hurling her from her office. She hugged her, hoping to ease the girl's awkwardness and pain, even though her own pain was slicing through her like a knife.

"I'll be okay soon, sweetie. Don't worry about your performance review. It's going to come out all right. You'll be happy. I promise."

Shonda brightened. She swiped at a falling teardrop. "Thanks, Tawney. I'm here if you need me." She stepped from the office.

Before Tawney could recuperate, Dominique St. James, her best friend, stuck her head in the door. "You gonna make it girlfriend?" She hugged Tawney.

"Domi." Tawney used her pet nickname for Dominique. "I need a cigarette in the worst way and some fresh air. Let's get out of this building. Can you break?"

"Yeah. Let's go."

Outside the building strolling along, Tawney lit her cigarette, taking fast, short puffs. Dominique observed this but didn't say anything.

They walked along for a while before Tawney said, "Dominique, I feel like I'm living in a nightmare. My only child has been gunned down like a dog in the streets. And I don't know why. And then some boy got killed at Jazz's funeral. You saw that. And someone brought his body to Shannon."

"I didn't see who it was because Shannon was on top of me. There was so much confusion. But I can't escape the feeling that . . ." Tawney took a long drag from the cigarette. She stopped walking.

"What?" Dominique said.

"I don't know. I thought Shannon had really changed. But lately I just don't know. What if he's been doing things I don't know about? What if his past or present has cost me my child? I don't know that I can live with that, Domi." Scalding tears rolled down Tawney's cheeks.

Dominique gathered her in her arms. "It's going to be okay. Just cry it out, girlfriend. You're entitled. Don't you ever forget that you're entitled."

Dominique sincerely hoped that Shannon's bad attitude and street antics hadn't cost them the life of little Jasmine Davenport.

Chapter II

Shannon walked over to the neighborhood nightclub called the Dome. The glittering lights flashed above a neon sign that had the club's name on it. It was a tightly built structure with a glass dome top. He could see the kaleidoscope of colors reflecting through the glass roof.

He reached in his jacket pocket for a cigarette. He lit it with his monogrammed lighter. The one Tawney gave him for his birthday. Just looking at it reminded him of her. Her pain over the loss of Jazz was wrapping around him like a blanket. Her pain mingled with his own, felt like a hollow hole in his chest.

He pushed open the door to the club. He stood inside adjusting his eyes to the smoky, dusky atmosphere before approaching the bar. Smokey, who had been the bartender for as long as Shannon could remember, hurried over to him.

People were playing pool and watching TV. The jukebox was playing on a low volume.

"Sorry about Jazz," Smokey said before Shannon could speak.

Shannon looked around the club. "Yeah, man. But death doesn't automatically end things. You know what I mean?"

Smokey nodded.

He poured some gold liquid from a bottle of Jack Daniel's in a glass. He passed it to Shannon. Shannon downed it in one shot.

He put the glass on the counter. Smokey automatically refilled it. "Yeah. I know."

Shannon looked at him closely, taking another sip from the glass. "What's the word? My past is haunting me, man. I need answers."

Shannon drained the glass. He snuffed out the cigarette. Smokey refilled it. He leaned close to Shannon, after taking a quick look around. "Michael Claybay is T-Bone's brother. T-Bone works for Rico. A bottle of this"—Smokey lifted the Jack Daniel's bottle—"will loosen his tongue. Nothing happens in this city that he don't know about."

Smokey lifted his head toward Michael where he was sitting at the end of the bar drinking cheap wine. "You know him, right? From back in the day?"

"Yeah. I know Michael and I know Rico, who's a stupid young street punk with nothing better to do than hang out on street corners."

Shannon lit a cigarette; he swigged from the Jack Daniel's bottle.

Smokey shook his head. "Rico used to be that. Now he's a dangerous, deadly young entrepreneur who's getting serious paid. He's clocking, man. No joke. If you ain't noticed, my man has lost his puberty."

Shannon narrowed his eyes. "Is that right? No more gang-banging?"

Smokey wiped the bar nervously. "He's graduated. Turf wars. High stakes and lots of green stuff with Solomon's Temple pictured on the back."

He hit a button on the cash register, pulling out a dollar bill. He pointed to the temple on the back. "Solomon was a wealthy and wise man. These boys ain't wise and they want to be wealthy. A dangerous combination."

Shannon swigged a long, healthy gulp directly from the bottle. He pulled a hundred-dollar bill from his pocket, handing it to Smokey. "Here you go, man."

Smokey refused. "This one's on the house, man. I'm buying."

He gave a slight imperceptible nod toward Michael Claybay, and then moved on to serve other customers.

Shannon made his way down the bar to Michael. He sat on the stool next to him, plopping the bottle of Jack Daniel's between them. Michael eyed the bottle with appreciation. He was a skinny little dude with a fast, quirky way of talking.

"What's up, Michael?"

"You black. Sorry about your kid."

Shannon slid the bottle over to him along with his glass. Michael poured. He swallowed the liquor in one gulp.

"Yeah," Shannon said. "Me too. Drink up. A man with a lost child doesn't like to drink alone. You know what I mean?"

Michael poured another shot. He downed it. Then another. They sat in the kind of companionable silence one can only find in a bar.

After a while Michael fidgeted in his seat. He poured another glass. He reached in his pocket, pulling out a pack of cigarettes, searching for a light. Shannon gave him his lighter.

He lit up quickly, inhaling deeply. "So what brings you out? Ain't seen you on the streets for a long while." He leaned back in his chair. He cast an eye on the game on the overhead TV, even though the sound was turned down.

Shannon studied him before replying. "Answers, man."

"About?"

"Jasmine."

Michael shrugged callously as the liquor surged through his body, creating a comfort level, taking control. "What's there to know? She's dead, right?"

It was all Shannon could do to keep from knocking him out of the seat. But this would not be a wise move. At least not yet.

"I need to know why she's dead."

Michael downed another glass. He immediately refilled the glass. He grinned at Shannon. Shannon flicked open his jacket. He gently fingered a roll of bills. He never looked at Michael.

"So what if I knew a tidbit or two? What would be in it for me?"

"Cold hard cash good enough?"

"Depends on how much."

"Two G's."

Michael ran his tongue around the rim of the glass, savoring the taste of the liquor. "All right."

"Start talking."

The club was starting to come to life around them, and so did Michael Claybay by way of a lethal tongue. "Word is, Rico's boy Temaine flipped to the other side. He's tired of being an underling to Rico. He's hooking up with Ballistic undercover. More profits, less fear, because Ballistic's one nasty mother. He's Rico's most dangerous rival. The man put the D in danger. Trust me on this. Anyway, he wants it all. The turf and the profits."

Michael pushed the glass away finally. His jaw twitched. Shannon was silent.

"Rico found out about Temaine. He hired Spence Parkinson to hit Temaine. A little cash independent contract. Spence was an independent hit man. For the right price."

He shrugged. "Anyway, it would look like an everyday rival hit. No big deal, right? Rico is about the money and ain't getting shut out a' no profits, right?"

Shannon nodded. "Right."

"Except something goes wrong and Jasmine gets hit, seriously jeopardizing Rico's position." Michael shifted. He pulled the glass closer again, taking another sip.

Pure malice leaped from Shannon's eyes, but Michael was oblivious of it. "Only the tables turned on Rico because the word is that Ballistic hired Spence to hit Rico, which means that Rico paid for a hit he was never gonna get. Spence double-crossed Rico."

Michael drained the glass. "Rico's running scared. So he kills two birds with one stone. One, he has Spence taken out. Two, he sends a powerful message to Ballistic that he ain't rolling over. A declared war. He pays props for Jazz's death by taking down her killer. He's still got time to take care of Temaine. He ain't suspicious. He thinks the hit was on Rico." Michael shrugged.

Shannon beckoned for a glass. He poured a stiff shot, sipping from the liquor. "There's more."

A nervous tick jumped in Michael's jaw. "Rico wants you out of the way. You're a liability he can't afford to worry about. One he didn't anticipate on having. An angry father with the police watching him."

Michael took another sip. He raised his eyebrows at Shannon. "Didn't your house get hit?" He stood up. He picked up the cigarettes and lighter from the bar, putting them in his pocket.

Shannon glared sparks of hatred at him. They locked gazes. Michael finally got a sense of something being wrong, off kilter and out of balance, through the alcoholic haze he was floating in. "I can't afford no leaks, man, or my life ain't worth two cents."

Shannon stood up. He laid two cents on the counter for Michael. "That would be deadly justice."

Michael looked at the two pennies. "Yo, man, this ain't what we discussed, you son of a—"

Shannon dropped him with a fast right to the jaw. He stepped over him to walk to the men's room. Down the bar, Smokey frowned at the scene.

Chapter 12

After leaving that nigga Michael Claybay lying in his tracks cold-cocked, Shannon walked down the street in a self-inflicted fog.

The pain was so deep about losing his daughter that it sliced through him in white-hot spasms of flashing electrical currents. He thought he might get lost in this void and never come back.

He leaned against a pole and doubled over as another spasm shot through his stomach. As he dry-heaved he realized that just this simple act provided some comfort. At least it provided a physical outlet for his hurt and despair.

He could deal with the physical. It was what he knew best.

He wiped his mouth, standing up straight. He had changed his life for that little girl. From the moment he had laid eyes on her, he realized his life would never be the same. He had ceased to be a criminal, just like that.

His daughter upon her birth had skin the color of a chocolate-brown mink, with shining bright eyes. Her eyes shone like new money, as they used to say. He had considered her a prize, and had treated her like one.

The instant she had looked at him the bond had been set. It was he, not Tawney, who had gotten up for her feedings at night, changed her, cradled her in his arms, and sung nursery rhyme songs to her in his off-key baritone.

He hadn't wanted his daughter to grow up without a strong male figure for support. There were too many black kids who grew up without ever knowing their fathers, or having any type of positive relationship with them.

So he and Tawney had virtually switched roles. He had become the stay-at-home dad, and Tawney had pursued her career. Tawney was not the domestic type in the slightest sense of the word, so it was all good.

He had decided then and there that he wouldn't be in the streets when his daughter needed him. Nor would he be in jail, where her first glimpse of him would be like looking at a caged animal. He vowed that she would never see him through the vertical bars.

Or view his body in a casket, because of some street mishap. The only way he could ensure that was to get out of the streets and get out for good, and so he had.

After settling debts, putting cash aside, and severing all street connections, he had become in every sense of the word a daddy. In truth he had been both Daddy and Mommy to Jazz in many ways, because Tawney was always busy climbing the corporate ladder, career building or networking, trying to reach the next rung on the ladder.

However, it was an arrangement that made them both happy, and one that worked well for their small family. He loved being there for his daughter. He realized with another sharp pain that Jazz had been the only thing in his life that he had ever loved purely.

He loved the shine of her eyes, her twinkling smile. The way she threw her arms around his neck at night when he read her stories. He could still feel the soft, warm bubble bath smell rising up from her childlike innocence.

Hell, he had even learned how to braid her hair, make ponytails, and tie red ribbons in it. The two of them loved red ribbons. Jazz had been his image of the perfect little girl, almost like a storybook fantasy come true, and he had been a part of creating her.

Dear Jesus, how he missed her.

An unbidden image floated into his mind, as he remembered noticing that one of her ribbons was missing as she lay on the white hospital sheets, in a pool of blood, lifeless. He remembered thinking that the figure lying there couldn't be his child. But it was.

How ironic that he had lost his only child to the streets, after fleeing the streets so he wouldn't lose her. The sins of the fathers visited upon the children. Oh God, if he could only take it all back.

With that thought a flood of tears rolled unstoppable down his cheeks. No one would have believed it. At one time he had been considered one of the most dangerous, lethal criminals on the streets. No one dared cross him. He was what the old-school rappers called an Original Ganster, an O.G. in every sense of the word.

On this night he was a man with a dead child, lost to him forever. A howl of wounded anger, frustration, and loss echoed across Central Avenue. It sounded like it came from a stranger. He sat on the curb, hugging himself, rocking and crying like a baby. He couldn't believe she was gone. Not his Jazz. She couldn't be gone.

He was a man who had survived gunshot wounds, stabbings, gang beatings, the police, the system, and any number of contracts that had been put out on his life.

For the first time he wondered if he would survive the death of his daughter. This was the one thing he didn't know if he would make it through.

Without realizing he was going to he yelled out loud, "Aw, Jesus, why'd you have to take her? Why?"

Engulfed in waves of pain he decided to pray. He hadn't prayed since before the night Jazz was murdered. He prayed for the resting of her soul in peace. This child he loved so much.

A branch swayed in the wind over his head. Shannon looked up. He could have sworn he'd heard his daughter's voice. Grief-stricken, he knew he was really losing it. Right next to his ear, he had felt Jazz's soft breath whispering, "Daddy, don't cry. I'm here, Daddy."

Shannon bowed his head between his legs. He knew as long as he lived, he would forever hear her voice.

Chapter 13

The following day Rico, Temaine, and Milkbone, another one of Rico's crew members, sat in Rico's Jeep on Springdale Avenue watching a hot dice game being played out on the avenue. Money was spread out all over the ground. There was lots of shoving, yelling, and rivalry going on.

Rico moodily stared out the window of his Jeep. "Them niggas don't ever get tired of ripping each other off."

Temaine burst out in laughter. "That's because they ain't got no real cash kicking in. It's the way of the world. What you ain't got you take. Them niggas be real bored, man."

Milkbone cleared his throat. "Temaine, you never fail to surprise me. I know by now you heard Ballistic is going ballistic. You know what I mean? And here you sit like you ain't got a care in the world laughing at some silly niggas instead of spreading a plan that's gonna keep this wacko at bay."

Disgusted, he hit the back of Temaine's seat. "You is one amazing nigga, man."

Rico shot Milkbone a cold glance through the rearview mirror. "Chill, my man. Ain't nobody ignoring that fool. Just ain't nobody worrying about him either."

Temaine jumped in. He was livid with anger. "And why don't you get on the right page, Milkbone? Shannon Davenport is being harassed by the police right now because his daughter's dead, and because his house got shot up."

"Which means, you dense-ass nigga, he may be looking for some answers of his own. And niggas like Ballistic used to wet their pants at the sound of his name back in the day. He's a legend. An O.G., man, that nigga created the game we're playing. You with that?"

Rico sighed. He banged his hand on the steering wheel. Temaine with his two faces was making him sick. He couldn't believe he had grown up and been best friends with this double-crossing weasel. He was a walking dead man. This punk was going to find out soon that Rico knew that the only allegiance he paid was to the almighty dollar.

He actually sounded like he looked up to Shannon Davenport. He was worshipping that old-school punk in his presence. The only name on the streets of Newark that was gonna inspire fear and awe was his. Temaine would know that soon enough.

Not ready to lay his cards on the table yet, Rico said, "Shannon Davenport is a liability I can't afford. He won't be around long. He's going to be one less mama's son. Believe that. I'm gonna do him. In the right time and in the right place. The police are all over him."

Milkbone grimaced. "When?"

Rico locked gazes with him in the rearview mirror. "I don't answer to you, Milkbone. When I'm ready and when I say so. That's when." He spat out the car window.

Milkbone rolled his eyes, staring out the window, avoiding further eye contact with Rico. "You know what? I didn't mean nothing by the question. I was just asking. I'm out of here. Okay?"

Milkbone hit the door handle on the Jeep. He stepped out. Just as he did his attention was drawn to a shadow on the roof. But it was too late. An eerie, weird keening sound exploded in the moment of silence.

A voice with a surreal sound to it, distinctly sang, "Rockabye, baby."

The barrel of the gun that was pointed at Milkbone kicked off a shot, dropping him in his own blood. The crowd on the street dissipated. Skilled in the menaces of the hood, they knew the drill and they were immediately ghost.

Rico hit the ignition as he watched smoke drift up from Milkbone's slain body. The Jeep lurched forward. Milkbone's body got caught under the tire as the Jeep sped away, dragging the body along with it. It finally shook loose, lying facedown in scattered blood all over the street.

Aisha Jackson, Jazz's friend, stood wide-eyed holding on to her bedroom curtain. The little girl's body shook as she stared through the curtain at the familiar figure. She was so scared she couldn't move.

She had just witnessed her first murder. She stared in the eyes of the murderer. He smiled. What held Aisha frozen in her spot was not the person she saw shoot Milkbone.

Aisha was used to hearing gunshots, as well as police and emergency vehicles screeching through the night, in her neighborhood. She had even witnessed her friend Jazz die. And she knew the shooter was a bad man.

What held her scared stiff, and trembling in her spot, was what she saw standing just behind the murderer. She blinked, hoping to open her eyes and find it gone.

When she opened her eyes the shooter was gone, but riveted to the spot just beyond where the shooter had stood was the one who didn't leave. The one who didn't smile. It was the one who had come to stay.

The one who would rock all of their cradles before it was all said and done. "Rockabye, baby," it sang. The lyrics fell like the impending doom they were in the midst of.

Aisha dropped the curtain. She backed away. She half expected it to appear in front of her. But it didn't. At least it didn't on this night.

The little girl climbed into her bed. She pulled the covers over her head. The only sound in the room was that of her teeth chattering. She might have gone to tell her mother except that her vocal cords had been temporarily stricken. She couldn't speak.

The only movement in the room was her trembling body. And the Darkling wasn't worried because it knew she would never speak again.

Chapter 14

Across the street from Aisha Jackson's house an old woman known as Mama sat in her spot by the window, peeking out from behind her shade. Only on this night she wished she hadn't. Sometimes you were better off not seeing things.

Mama and Papa, as they were respectively known, had lived in the Central Ward for close to fifty years and had grown old there in their time. Mama was a spry eighty and Papa was eighty-two.

Papa had always warned Mama about being at that window. He'd admonished her, telling her that when people always looked for things, sometimes they saw things they didn't want to see. But Mama had paid no heed to the old coot, because he'd never know a thing if it wasn't for her.

His nose was always stuck in that newspaper or on a Yankees game. He couldn't care less what happened on the streets. Mama, on the other hand, was very perceptive—sensitive to certain things. Because of this secondary sense her world was a much broader one than Papa's.

Papa looked over at Mama and he didn't like what he saw. "Mama, I told you to stay away from that window." He had heard the shots. "What's wrong?" The hair on the back of his arms was bristling.

When Mama turned to him he knew there had been a subtle

shift in things. He didn't cotton much to all the nonsense about senses and all that, but within himself he did have a healthy respect for Mama's sight.

In fact he had a li'l of it himself, but it didn't make no sense to go around spouting that kind of stuff to people. They didn't believe in much of anything these days.

Besides, he much preferred dealing with things he could see. Even if they showed up in the form of gats and Uzis. Breaking out of his reverie he gazed at Mama, shut his eyes, and then opened them to find there was no change.

The whites of Mama's eyes was all he could see. Her eyes were rolled up in the back of her head.

Spittle was forming in the corner of her mouth. Papa hobbled over to her as fast as his eighty-two years would allow. Gently he touched her arm. He knew that fast movements might lock her in the trance for longer than he wanted.

"What's wrong, Mama?" he repeated, trying to penetrate her psyche.

Mama blinked. Her eyes rolled back to their proper place. She looked at Papa as though she couldn't see him, but could only feel that he was there. "They done shot Milkbone. He's dead."

Mama knew all the players.

She had fed and clothed enough of these kids over time when their no-good sorry mamas had preferred getting high to feeding and clothing their kids. She had seen enough of them trading their food stamps for drugs, letting their kids go hungry.

Papa waited. He knew there was more. He felt it in his bones. In fact his left knee was throbbing. That never happened unless something more than what was on the surface was going on.

"Aisha Jackson, that precious little darling, was in her window, Papa. She done saw the whole thing. Why was she in her window?"

Papa didn't know how to answer so he remained quiet, like the still waters he had been reared in. He was a quiet man by nature, one who observed more than he spoke.

"It's here, Papa. That's why all this killing's going on. Our people don't understand their spirits is being traded."

Papa put an arm around her shoulder. Slowly but surely he guided her away from the window over to the couch. Mama looked at Papa. She swallowed hard before saying, "It done took Aisha's speech. That girl's in trouble. We've got to get it back."

Papa definitely didn't like the sound of this one. It reminded him of the swamps of Louisiana many a year ago. Sometimes when the realms or spirits as they are known to some people were fixing to act up this was the kind of stuff you heard. Problem was, these people in the North didn't know nothing about that.

And he knew today's kids were wide-open vessels to the magic of darkness. They didn't have nothing to fight with. Finally Papa couldn't hold his peace. He spoke. "Mama, what's that you saw?"

"It."

Papa sighed. "What'd it say?"

Mama stared at him as though he'd done lost his mind. A shiver raced up her back. "It said rockabye, baby, Papa."

Papa froze.

Before Mama could utter another word, he reached for his gilt-paged Bible.

Chapter 15

Rico paced his basement while Temaine sucked on his licorice. There was a knock on the door. Rico pulled his gun from his shoulder holster.

Kesha appeared in the doorway. "Michael Claybay, T-Bone's brother, is here. He wants to see you. He says it's important."

Rico holstered the gun. "Send him down."

A moment later Michael walked in. He glanced nervously at Temaine. "I got some information for you. It's gonna cost you two G's."

Rico reached into his pocket. He flicked the bills into Michael's hand without asking any questions.

Michael stared greedily at the bills, before snatching them out of Rico's hand. "Shannon Davenport is gonna take you out. He's got it in his mind that you're responsible for his daughter's death." Michael's jaw twitched.

"Is that right?" Rico glanced at Temaine.

Michael's voice was fast and clipped. "It is."

Rico nodded. "And how do you know this?"

"He told me."

"And what did you tell him?"

Michael glanced nervously at the floor. "Nothing. I don't know nothing. What could I say?"

Rico nodded. "Do you know where I can find him?"

Michael laughed. Temaine stopped sucking on his licorice. He watched Michael with interest.

"Yeah. The Dome."

Rico peeled off ten one-hundred-dollar bills. He shoved them into Michael's hand. "You're on my payroll as of now. Let's go."

Michael visibly relaxed. He smiled.

Rico looked at Temaine. "I said let's go."

The Dome was in high gear. It was jumping. Shannon sat alone at the bar, sipping Jack Daniel's. Shonda walked in, standing by the door, adjusting her eyes to the dark. Looking around she spotted Shannon Davenport alone at the bar.

She was dressed in a short gold dress, with matching gold heels. Her legs were oiled and accented to perfection. An air of seduction clung to her like a second skin as she tossed long blond-weaved braids over her shoulder.

She walked straight up to Shannon, tapping him on the shoulder. "Don't I know you?" she said in a lilting, sensual, husky voice that dripped with an invitation to anywhere he wanted to go.

Shannon showed no trace of memory. But appreciation leaped into his eyes. "Do you?"

A slow caressing smile displayed itself across Shonda's lips. "Yeah. We met at the office party last year in the bank. You're Tawney's husband, right?"

Shannon glared at her. She'd ticked a nerve without meaning to.

"I'm Shannon Davenport, if that's what you mean."

Shonda traced a polished nail down his arm, quickly recovering, saying sweetly, "Shannon Davenport. That is exactly what I meant."

Shannon smiled, chiding himself for taking out his bad temper on this gorgeous, specimen of a female. Looking into her eyes, a glimmer of recognition nudged him. "Yeah, I remember you now. You look different without your bank clothes on."

Shonda returned his smile. "I have a life outside of the bank."

He gave her a once-over. "Is that so?"

She returned his gaze. "It is."

Switching gears, Shonda laced her voice with just the right amount of sentiment. "I'm sorry about your daughter. That's real messed up."

Shannon nodded as the familiar ache squeezed his chest.

"May I sit down?"

"Yeah."

She sat next to him, placing her hand warmly over his. He felt the warmth against his chilled hand, and decided he liked it. How long had it been since Tawney had reached for his hand?

"If there's anything I can do for you and Tawney, please let me know."

"I will. What are you drinking?"

"Hennessey. Straight up."

Shannon signaled Smokey. "That's a strong drink."

"I'm a strong lady."

Smokey arrived in front of them.

"Give the lady a Hennessey. Straight up."

Smokey poured the drink. Before he could finish pouring, shattered glass came raining down through the roof of the club. A body hit the floor with a thud. People screamed and scrambled to get out of the club. The music came to an abrupt halt.

A man's body, bound and gagged, lay in the middle of the floor. Shannon shot out of his seat, making his way to the body. His eyes widened in disbelief as he stared down at the blood-filled lifeless eyes of Michael Claybay.

There was a piece of paper attached to the body. Chaos reigned supreme in the club. Shannon looked around to see if anyone was looking. Satisfied that there was enough confusion going on, he unpinned the paper. It had three thousand dollars in bills attached.

The note read *You're next*.

Shannon broke out in a sweat. He balled the note up in his hand. Shonda tapped him on the shoulder. "Come on. We need to get out of here."

He didn't move.

Shonda took his hand. "Come on!"

In the midst of the night Shannon left with the femme fatale, ignoring the one word that screamed through his mind. That word was, *don't!* He could no longer hear anything except the blood pounding in his ears.

It was on. And it was on in the biggest way. Slowly, he felt his salvation slip from his grasp. Replacing it was a murderous, vengeful rage.

Heed my earlier warning about seeing with your spirit and not just with your eyes. Vengeance spawns darkness, and in the darkness there is no light. The Serpent's head is reared even when you cannot see it.

Chapter 16

Shannon followed Shonda up to the porch of the shabby two-family house. The house was in desperate need of some repairs, but Shannon barely noticed it.

He needed to put a plan together to stop the madness that was surrounding him. Shonda fumbled for her keys. Locating them she stuck the key in the lock, revealing a living room that was as shabby as the outside of the house.

Apparently while she liked to be in the streets dressed to the nines, this particular attitude hadn't extended itself to her sleeping quarters.

Every stick of furniture in the room was old and worn. Paint was peeling off the ceilings. Shannon was in a fog; the surroundings barely registered a blip in his mind's eye. Shonda tugged on his arm, pulling him forward to meet her nana mama.

"Nana Mama, this is my friend Shannon. Shannon, this is Nana Mama."

Shannon extended a hand toward the old woman, wondering at the brightness of her eyes and the folds of lined skin falling from her face. She was an interesting-looking woman, who looked like she could've been around for more than a century. "Nice to meet you, Nana Mama."

Nana Mama sized him up quickly, her eyes penetrating and

alert. "You too, young man. Any friend of Shonda's is a friend of mine. Make yourself at home."

The smell of homemade apple pie reached Shannon's nostrils, along with what smelled like collard greens. Nana Mama, noticing he had smelled her cooking, smiled.

"My nana mama's the best cook in the hood, Shannon."

He replied politely. "I'll bet she is."

Meanwhile a picture of Michael Claybay's body falling through showers of glass flashed in his mind.

"You're welcome to have something to eat," Nana Mama said.

Shonda shot her a nasty look. "Later, Nana Mama. I'm gonna show Shannon my room."

Nana Mama eyed Shannon once again. "Well, he's a good-looking young buck."

Shannon blushed, his skin flushing warm. The old woman smiled again, knowing she had hit her target. She hoped Shonda had landed one with some money for a change. They could sure use it around here.

Nana Mama wasn't too crazy about that other boy Shonda had latched on to. He was what Nana Mama called death-struck. You could see it in his eyes.

She sighed. She knew her granddaughter didn't have near enough sense to key into what she was thinking.

Shonda turned to Shannon, her eyes animated from the heat of wanting him. "Let's go."

There were no preliminaries with her. She had always gone after exactly what she wanted and gotten it. Shannon followed her up to the bedroom. Perhaps he could drown his pain, even if it was in the arms of a stranger for one night.

Tomorrow would be a different day.

Proverbs 2:16: To deliver thee from the strange woman, even from the stranger which flattereth with her words.

Chapter 17

The following morning a bleary-eyed Rico, along with Temaine, who looked rested compared to Rico, went out to climb into the Jeep.

Rico threw the keys to Temaine. "You drive."

Temaine caught the keys. He pressed the button for the automatic door lock. Pulling the door open he jumped back. On the seat of the Jeep was Eight Ball's head. There was no body to go along with it. His vacant eyes stared out at Temaine as though he could actually see him.

Rico's cell phone rang. He answered while wondering at the shocked expression on Temaine's face. "Yeah?"

A deep raspy voice emanating chords of darkness snaked its way through the phone lines. "Rico, my boy. Why don't you look and see what has your boy in shock?"

Rico looked around. He didn't see anyone. The streets were practically deserted at this time of the morning. All the night players were shut in, keeping the light out of their eyes until time for the evening's business.

Rico peered into the Jeep. He saw Eight Ball's head residing on the plush leather of his seat. "You son of a—"

Ballistic cut him off. "In the future, Mr. Rico, you will have to learn to find better hiding places for your friends. This is the only time I'm going to change your Pampers, baby boy." The phone went dead in Rico's ear.

Rico bugged out. He kicked the Jeep door in a rage, until a dent appeared. "That punk-ass nigga is insane." Rico surveyed the area. He motioned to Temaine to do something about the head in the Jeep. Temaine grimaced.

"This punk done lost his mind, man," Temaine said. "We're gonna have to pump up the volume."

Rico nodded.

Rico's mind was working overtime. He would definitely have to turn the heat up under Ballistic. And it would have to be lightning quick. His Cuban connect had already questioned him, word having reached him through the grapevine of a war on the streets.

Rico had assured him it was all under control. The connect would move quickly to displace him if there was a problem, and he knew it. All they cared about was the bottom dollar. Who was controlling the turf in Newark didn't mean jack to them. They would supply whoever was holding it down.

He needed a grandstand move, one that would solidify his stronghold. But first he would toy with this nigga. He would show him that he hadn't uprooted him with Eight Ball's death.

Jasmine Davenport's funeral had definitely given a nigga one up. Dropping Spence in her grave would be a legend that would live on the streets for years to come.

Rico was always one to top even himself, and he knew just the thing. He had been running things since he was what the old-timers called a piss spot on the sheets. But now he had risen. He was going to set the standards for these niggas. When his name rang they were going to know to bow down.

Rico didn't have to wait long to recreate himself. The opportunity presented itself at Spence's funeral services. Outside the church on Clinton Avenue vehicles were stacked and packed, triple-parked along the streets.

All had come to pay homage to one of the fallen in the game. There were enough Cadillac Escalades on the block to stock a showroom.

The hearst and a line of black limousines were lined up at the head of the block, so as to lead the procession from the church. The ghetto was glistening and glittering on this day. There was enough gold, diamonds, Versace, and Prada in the house to make Fifth Avenue proud.

Tiffany's window display of diamonds and rubies was front and center on the women who had players that were getting real paper.

Funerals in the hood had become like hot spots for the latest nightclub. It was less about a life being lost, and more about who was who, who appeared to be connected because their face was seen in the place, as well as who was with whom and who had on the latest gear.

It was the perfect spot for the spectacle that was about to go down. Rico and his crew parked directly in the middle of the street, in front of the church. Soft music floated out onto the streets.

Rico jumped out of his Jeep, and the crew followed, their guns drawn. He strutted up to the doors of the church, pulling them open arrogantly.

Stepping inside the church, the crew looked like an ensemble from the *Men in Black* movie. They were all dressed down in black silk suits, with matching black brims, black leather ankle-length coats and gloves, with black sunglasses sporting gold Dolce & Gabbana emblems on the side.

Everyone had a Glock that was drawn, with the exception of Rico, who stood in the lead. The infrared lights on the Glocks crisscrossed the pews, landing on the preacher's chest, creating a patchwork effect of infrared light.

There was a stunned silence. Everything came to a halt as Rico locked eyes with the minister, who was standing behind the pulpit, presiding over the coffin.

Not breaking eye contact Rico strolled down the aisle. Stopping in the middle of the aisle, his crew spread out around the church. It was a well-orchestrated move, conducted by a street master. Rico glared his hatred, venom spilling from his very pores at the seated mourners.

The mourners were scared. Some of the minor rivals who were in the house to show their respect were not happy with being caught short. If anything broke out, Rico had the advantage. They were quickly tallying up their tabs, evaluating whether or not they would be in the line of fire.

Once the crew was in place Rico continued his leisurely stroll until he reached the coffin. He looked inside at Spence's body. Somebody had spent top dollar with the undertaker because the hole they had blown in Spence's head was barely visible.

That meant somebody had spread serious paper. Rico wondered at the source. Again Temaine's double-crossing ways surfaced in his mind, pushing Ballistic out of the forefront. Red flames of rage passed before his eyes.

Not a sound could be heard in the church. Even the music had stopped playing. The only thing you could hear was breathing, as though all the guests had taken one collective breath.

Rico leaned over the coffin. He spat in Spence's dead face. A woman let loose with a high-pitched scream that scraped against the stained-glass windows of the church, and echoed back to the audience in sheer pain.

Others were yelling and crying. Rico snapped his fingers. Some of the crew convened on the coffin. The woman who screamed was Spence's mother. She thought she was going to pass out.

Not only had she lost one of her sons, but also his body was being violated right in front of her eyes. It was the work of the devil. She had been a God-fearing woman all of her life. She was a faithful follower of Jesus Christ.

She had not, however, been able to instill these values in her sons. Try as she might she had lost the battle. They wanted everything now. They resented poverty. They wanted to be rich and powerful.

She was unable to bear the humiliation and deep-rooted pain of yet another intrusion from children she didn't know, who displayed antics that were usually only reported when countries were at war.

She had had her children late in life. She was living in a time that was as foreign to her as a faraway land. When she was a child, adults spoke and children listened. She never thought she'd see the day when black people had to fear their own kids. Their own blood was turning against them, and they had lost every ounce of respect.

For a brief moment she remembered the scene from *The Greatest Story Ever Told* when Christ was on his way to the cross, heading to his own crucifixion. People were weeping. He had stopped in front of a woman and said, "Do not weep for me; weep for that which is coming forth from your wombs."

Closing her eyes with a pain as sharp as that from a straight-edged razor, she now understood those words. The black women of America had their own crosses to bear.

She and many other mothers were rearing, or had reared, children, who were bearing fruits of evil that they couldn't live with. It was beyond her comprehension. This hoodlum standing in front of her was the final straw.

Unable to bear any more she decided to beg, anything to appeal to this young man, to stop this madness. It was just too much.

Lord knows she had tried to raise these boys right. She was a single parent with little in the way of economics. She had given them the best she had, but had lost them to the streets anyway.

Today she was burying one of them. She shouldn't have to endure more than that.

She managed to stand though her legs were wobbly. Her knees were shaking. She was sure everyone could hear them knocking together. Especially Shonda, who had stood up on the side of her for support.

"Please," she said.

She found the strength to look directly in Rico's eyes. Nothing but black waves of hatred emanated in an electrical current that she would have found hard to believe if she hadn't experienced it.

Trying to connect she looked behind the depths of Rico's eyes. There was nothing there. Knowing it would be to no avail she stated her case anyway.

"Please. Please don't do this."

Rico spat at her feet. He looked coldly in her eyes. "Your son doesn't deserve your pleas."

"In the name of Jesus," she said.

Rico gave her a look that would have shriveled her had she not known the power of the name she called on. And she would never know that in that blink of a second she had been one step away from being dead herself, as Rico was just about to give the signal. Many of the lights from the infrared Glocks had been trained on her from the moment she stood up.

Rico twitched for the slightest of seconds. It was so minor it wasn't even noticed. Refraining from giving the order that would turn Spence's mother into the equivalent of Swiss cheese, he simply said, "Your son doesn't deserve the Lord's blessing, lady."

He gave a signal indicating to his crew that this lady should be taken out of the crosshairs of fire. Instantly the Glocks were repositioned.

Feeling the slightest bit uncomfortable, but having shown his hand now, Rico took a step back from her. He snapped his fingers. "Get him out of here."

At the issue of the order, there was more screaming and hollering from the women. The crew removed the body from the coffin. Mercifully Spence's mother fainted. The crew moved down the aisle with Spence's body in tow. Rico pulled up the rear.

When he reached the church doors the minister's voice rang out through the hallowed walls. His voice was trembling with anger. "How dare you disrespect the house of the Lord in this way, young man? You will burn in hell for this."

Rico turned around slowly. He looked deep into the minister's eyes. He looked around the pews. Then he threw his arms in the air, spreading them wide. "I'm already burning in hell, Mr. Preacher Man. Look around. And so are you."

"You have no respect for the dead," the minister countered.

"I ain't got none for the living either."

Rico turned his back on the minister. He walked arrogantly out of the same doors through which he had made his entrance.

Yeah, he was a ghetto legend. And they knew that. They'd better never forget it either.

Later Spence's body would be found in Branch Brook Park, riddled with bullet holes lying under a tree.

Chapter 18

Shonda sat in a car borrowed from her friend Tia in the Bronx. The car would not be recognized in Jersey. She had been sitting in the car and watching for hours.

She watched as Tawney came out of the house, got in her car, and drove away. Shannon had been knocked out with a tranquilizer, and was sprawled out in her bed with Nana Mama keeping a close watch.

Now that she had a taste of Tawney's honey by sleeping with her man it was time for her next move. It was simple. She would destroy this heifer. She had a personal day off from work so she had nothing but time to concentrate on Tawney. One of these days she would pull this whore's hair out, strand by strand.

Patiently she waited another half hour, making sure Tawney didn't forget anything or return to the house for any reason. Once she was satisfied this wouldn't happen she exited the car. She crept around the side of the house, entered the back porch, and inserted her credit card in the lock. Hearing the click she smiled.

She walked through the tastefully decorated kitchen equipped with stainless steel counters and the latest in Cusinart cookware. The witch had everything. Shonda spotted a lipstick-stained cup of coffee sitting on the table.

Making herself comfortable Shonda sat at the table. She crossed her legs, sipping from the cold cup of coffee. She daydreamed, imagining Shannon coming up behind her, nuzzling her neck. She could feel his warm arms embracing her, his breath against her cheek, wanting her. She was secure in the knowledge that he was hers.

And only hers.

This thought knocked Shonda off balance and back to reality, as a coldness swept through her body, reminding her that he wasn't hers, at least not yet. Tiring of the game she got up, walking through the house until she came to a room with the door closed.

No doubt this was Jazz's room. She could feel the spirit of the girl child emanating through the closed door. She opened the door, not in the least bit surprised to find the room looking exactly as if Jasmine was only away at school and would return at the end of the day. Tawney was one stupid broad.

Entering the room she closed the door behind her. The room was, simply put, a fairy tale. Every little girl's dream, it was decorated in pink and white, with a lace-covered canopy bed. Shonda took note of the fact that while Tawney lived in the ghetto, she lived like a ghetto princess.

The inside of her house was in sharp contrast to what lay beyond on the streets. She was privileged. She was also living a lie, pretending to be one of them when she wasn't.

The bookcases were stacked with classic children's stories, all lined up for the little dead princess Jasmine. Shonda smiled knowing Jasmine wouldn't be reading any more of these books.

She walked over, picking up the various stuffed animals that were tucked away on shelves, looking like they belonged in an FAO Schwartz window. Who the hell did Tawney think she was fooling? She wasn't knocking down these kinds of dollars at the bank.

There were traces of real cash here. Hey, maybe the ice queen was tricking her way up the ladder. Shonda wouldn't put it past her. She wouldn't be the first woman who had slept her way to the top.

Growing bored Shonda left Jasmine's room, strolling down the hallway, which was lined with pictures of a smiling Shannon, Tawney, and Jasmine or just Shannon and Tawney. In some cases just Jazz was in the pictures, in the varying stages of growing up.

Turning up her nose, her face in a grimace, Shonda took a tube of lipstick from her purse and swiped it across the pictures with Shannon and Tawney. In each picture she obliterated Tawney's face, leaving only Shannon's intact.

That ought to let the heifer know where she stood. She wasn't all that. Continuing on her way she knew the next room she was looking at belonged to Shannon and Tawney. That was apparent by all the bullet holes plastering the walls. "Nice decorating," she murmured under her breath as she entered the room.

The next thing that caught her eye was the king-sized bed, which took up a good amount of space in the room. Plaster and white dusting from the ceiling and police were all over the bed, but still she'd revel in what she came for.

She went over to the bed, smelling the pillows, and sure enough she caught a whiff of Shannon's masculine scent. Lying down in the bed she snuggled against his pillow. She knocked the other pillow belonging to Tawney to the floor.

She lay there for a while inhaling Shannon's scent. Finally she got off the bed, heading to the closet. She looked through all of Tawney's clothes. Selecting a long floor-length nightgown, she undressed and put it on.

There. Now she could be Tawney completely. Back to the bed she went where she could bask in her fantasies undisturbed. She got up again rumbling through the shoes and found the matching slippers and housecoat to the sheer, silky nightgown set.

Then she stood in front of the mirror, arranging her hair in the style Tawney usually wore. Rearranging her makeup to duplicate Tawney's she was satisfied. Tawney always wore light makeup, barely a hint with a touch of gold at her lips.

Now she was ready. "Jazz!" Shonda called. "Jazz."

Where was that girl? How many times had she told her to come right away when she called? Shaking her head in an exact imitation of Tawney, she wandered out of the room back down the hallway to Jasmine's room.

"Jazz," she said as she mimicked the tone of Tawney's voice. "Didn't you hear me calling you?"

Sitting in a white wicker rocking chair was a big Raggedy Ann doll. Shonda went over to the doll. She took its hand. "Jasmine, it's story time. Didn't you hear me call you?"

She sat on the foot of the bed pulling the doll on her lap as she reached over for one of the fairy-tale books. She situated her so she was comfortable. "Don't you love when Mommy reads to you, Jazz? Reading is fundamental for all little girls, you know," she said, sounding just like a taped commercial of *What's America Reading?*

While Tawney spent the day at work, trying hard to focus on the tasks at hand with very little success, Shonda spent a day in her life, feeling what it was like to be her. For no reason at all a shiver ran through Tawney's body as though someone had walked over her grave.

Before leaving, Shonda erased all traces of her ever having been in the house, even the lipstick-smudged pictures, although it pained her to do that. She had enjoyed obliterating Tawney's image. But it would be stupid to leave them that way. And the one thing Shonda was not was stupid. She was smarter than Tawney with her manufactured, fake IQ.

She was so angry spittle formed in the corner of her mouth. She raked her long nails through the air, imagining it was Tawney's face. She could feel the flesh peeling away, Tawney's skin underneath her nails. She was tall but Shonda would cut her down to size.

Tawney was living her life; with her man and her daughter and with bold audacity she was living in what should have been her house.

She wasn't supposed to be living in what amounted to a run-down shack with some pissy old woman who couldn't make it to the bathroom half the time. Working some underpaid job, taking orders from the likes of Tawney. She should be living here with her man taking care of her.

Yeah, Tawney was living her life. But that was okay for now because that's all it was, for now. Shonda grabbed her head as an immense headache of huge proportions slammed against her brain.

All she heard over and over again was Tawney with her bragging rights. "Jazz did this and Jazz did that. Jazz did this and Jazz did that." That's all they heard at work, Tawney bragging about Jazz. Her office was filled with pictures of her. She acted like she had birthed the next first lady or something.

Yeah, yeah, yeah. That heifer had what was coming to her. And Shonda definitely wasn't finished with her yet. She and Shannon had some baby making to do.

When Shonda returned to her grandmama's house the hair on her arms prickled. She wasn't feeling the vibe.

Her grandmother took one look at her face, her heart sinking. She knew this face and she didn't like it. Shonda was what the old folks called out of herself. This was a side to her granddaughter that she feared, and that came straight from hell.

"Where's Shannon?"

Nana Mama flinched. "He done left, child."

"Left!" Shonda screamed. "I told you to watch him."

Tears appeared in the old woman's eyes. "I tried but he said he had to leave. Said he had a headache. I even offered him something to eat, but he ain't want nothing to eat."

Shonda's eyes flashed pure madness. A stream of volcanic power shot from their depths, connecting with Nana Mama. The old woman shrank back.

Shonda grabbed her, shaking her like a rag doll. "I told you not to let him leave!"

The old woman's teeth rattled. And all she could think was this child done came from the pit, the pits of hell.

She was too fragile to defend herself. Besides, she'd seen the raving maniac that emerged from Shonda once when she had tried. The girl had torn her whole house up and then made her clean it back up.

Shonda stopped shaking her. She spat words at her that were not to be disobeyed. "Go to your room! Now!"

She shook her again. "You stupid, stupid old woman!"

When Shonda released her Nana Mama limped to her room off the back of the kitchen with tears streaming down her face. She decided then and there to call Mama and go over there for some lunch; they needed to talk. Mama's keen sight and Papa's listening powers would set her straight.

Nana Mama heard glass breaking as Shonda took off her high-heeled pump and smashed everything that was glass in the living room.

In a fit of rage once again she destroyed Nana Mama's house. It wasn't the first time. However, this would mark a turning point, as Shonda was beginning day by day and more and more to live in the face that Nana Mama feared.

The volume on the audio is screaming loudly; only you can't make any adjustments to the knob, in the physical. You now need to dig deep in your spirit because what you've just heard is being listened to in a different realm. And you are not the only one *listening.*

I repeat, this world is in and of itself Out A' Order.

Chapter 19

Shannon walked through his house. It was giving him the creeps, though. That was the only word for it. A chill had started at the base of his neck, traveling down to the middle of his back.

He couldn't quite put his finger on it, but something was out of whack. As he walked through the house he felt a violation but didn't see anything out of the ordinary. Unknowingly he had narrowly missed Shonda's grand appearance and exit.

He went over to Pete's birdcage and tossed him some bird feed. If only Pete could speak other than what he'd been taught Shannon would have gotten an earful. As it was, Pete couldn't form sentences he hadn't been taught, and it was just as well, because Shannon's day was about to go from bad to worse.

Outside in front of Shannon's house Campbell and Lombardo were breaking camp to get to his door. Lombardo in particular was feeling himself this morning because they finally had Shannon Davenport exactly where they wanted him, which was in a sling.

Lombardo knocked loudly and rudely on the door. Shannon opened it. He shook his head, twisting his lips sarcastically as soon as he saw them. Why was he not surprised? "What do you want?" he said, not bothering to invite them in.

Lombardo shot back, "You." He held out a pair of handcuffs. "What the hell is this all about?"

"Michael Claybay," Campbell said. Unlike Lombardo he was not happy with these circumstances. Call it gut feeling but he just wasn't feeling a lot of things that were going on with Shannon. Something was foul in the East River, but he couldn't put his finger on it.

Lombardo, not wasting any more time, said, "You're under arrest for the murder of Michael Claybay." He stepped forward with the cuffs.

Shannon's face darkened, his eyes turned to slits, but he held out his wrists. Back in the day he would have busted a cap on this cop so quick he wouldn't have known what hit him.

Cops were notorious for watching and following people. But Shannon, coming from the gangster mentality, knew that thugs and criminals weren't the only people who could be followed and watched. He knew some cops were arrogant to a point that they put their own safety at risk, not realizing that their badges didn't make them superhumans.

However, this wasn't back in the day and he wasn't who he used to be. He wasn't where he wanted to be but he was a long way from where he used to be so these thoughts were futile. He would have to find another way to handle this situation.

He wasn't trying to pile up no body counts on his conscience unless it was self-defense. If that were the case, then he'd kill a man in a heartbeat.

So instead of what he thought he said, "I didn't kill Michael Claybay."

"Oh, really? You recognize this?" Lombardo replied. He showed Shannon his monogrammed lighter in a plastic bag. Shannon visibly flinched.

"Your fingerprints are all over it. In fact, so are your initials." This was like taking candy from a baby. A feeling of this being too easy overcame Lombardo, but he chose to ignore it.

Lombardo turned the bag around, making a display of looking at the lighter. "These are nice little gifts as long as you don't leave them on dead bodies. I surmise that Michael Claybay was already dead when he was dropped through the glass dome roof of the club. Very clever of you. Were you grandstanding? Care to explain?"

"Not to you."

"You have the right to remain silent. Anything you say can and will be used against you in a court of law. You have the right to an attorney. If you cannot afford one, one will be appointed to you by the courts."

Lombardo took pure glee in reading Shannon his Miranda rights. "Do you understand?"

"Yeah. I want to make a phone call."

"You can do it downtown," Campbell said.

Lombardo shook his head in disgust. "I knew it was only a matter of time before you slipped. Let's go."

They led him to the police car.

In his cell Shannon sat with his head between his legs trying to figure out where this was all going.

He knew Rico had killed Michael Claybay as a means of sending him a message. In the street life, snitches were the lowest of the lowest. They were dirt on the ground. Although everyone used them, from thugs to criminal enterprises to police, no one respected them.

Shannon felt bad that he had used Michael Claybay for information and therefore gotten him killed. A twinge of guilt pinched his conscience. Something that never would have happened back in the day. But it was a new day and Shannon was wrestling with who he used to be in the past, and the man he had become in the present.

He'd needed to find out why his daughter had been killed.

It should have been Rico lying in the cold ground dead instead of Jazz. Shannon's blood boiled every time he thought about it. Now this punk was threatening him. He was ready whichever way it went down. It was the way it had to be. The unspoken doctrine of the street code: Be ready. Always be ready.

He had to roll like that if he wanted to live.

Chapter 20

In Rico's basement the crew was shooting pool and playing the pinball machine. Rico and T-Bone stood off in a corner of the room talking.

Rico put his arm around Michael Claybay's brother, T-Bone, playing the game for all it was worth. "Michael's death is gonna be vindicated. We ain't going out like that," he said with a mixture of sincere sympathy and vengeance. "Have I ever let you down before?"

T-Bone shook his head. "Naw."

"And I ain't going to let you down now. You're my brother and you know that."

"Yeah, man, you're always there. I know you got a brother's back. I know that. But I ain't letting no bars separate me from Shannon Davenport, yo."

"Looka here. Don't even sweat that, man. If I have to I'll bond Shannon out just so you can have him. But there's one thing I've got to have your word on."

"What's that?"

"A man's word is his bond," Rico said.

T-Bone nodded. "Word is bond."

"You can rough him up but you can't take him out. He's mine."

T-Bone wrestled with this thought. He wanted Shannon in the

worst way and he didn't want any strings attached as to how he would get him. Rico told him Shannon had killed his brother, and revenge was in his heart.

Rico, on the other hand, needed to make an example out of Shannon. He wanted Shannon to represent the dust of an era long past. The O.G.'s. Leaving him as the one who brought in a new day.

He didn't have time for old-school punks trying to revitalize their names on the streets. Shannon's daughter was dead and that was that. Rico had paid props for that. He had a daughter of his own. Shannon should've gotten over it, but since he hadn't Rico would help him along.

Michael had been T-Bone's only brother. He'd always looked out for T-Bone when he was small and growing up. Although everyone knew he was a drunk, when it came to T-Bone he had played both mom and pop, always making sure he had what he needed even if it meant passing up a bottle or two.

Michael was blood. And as his grandfather used to say, blood is thicker than water. Nothing was supposed to come between you and your blood.

Rico, sensing T-Bone's reluctance to give his word on this, gripped him by the shoulders to drive his point home. "I'm serious, man. You've got to let me pay props for you. You're my boy. That's my heart to you, man. We family."

T-Bone sighed. He wasn't happy about it, but he looked up to Rico and he respected the ranks of the streets. If Rico caught a body for him, it would elevate his status in the crew, as well as with the other thugs on the street.

Rico's crew was the only other one besides Ballistic's that didn't have a street moniker. Rico was of the frame of mind that his crew was known by their actions and therefore didn't need a name. Ballistic, on the other hand, was the only name a person needed to know.

After evaluating the situation T-Bone finally said, "Yeah. Okay. You got it. But I ain't waiting too long. If Shannon's ass is not on the streets soon I'm going to make like a magician and penetrate them bars downtown to get him. You feeling me?"

"I feel you. Don't worry, you won't have to wait too long."

* * *

In the police station Lombardo was smiling. This was a day he had been waiting for. He was tired of catering to Shannon Davenport. He had an ill feeling about the cat-and-mouse game Campbell insisted on playing with him.

He'd grown up in Bloomfield, which wasn't that far from Newark. He knew how hard it was to make it. He hadn't been born with a silver spoon in his mouth.

But as far as he was concerned, being poor and black was no excuse for the insanity that spewed across Newark's streets, making victims of the hardworking people who didn't want any part of the madness. Those were the people he was there to protect as well as his own.

They definitely couldn't have the crime from Newark spilling over onto the streets of Bloomfield. Although every city had its problems in Bloomfield you would never see dealers, thugs, and lowlifes out on the corners kicking it like they owned the world.

Bloomfield didn't put up with that nonsense. If they tried that in his city, he knew darned well they would lock them up, give them fifty years, and throw away the key like it was nobody's business.

He considered it to be his job to at least keep it confined, if he couldn't control it. He didn't want that poison and the venomous attitudes that went with it in the town where his family resided.

Lombardo came out of his reverie as Campbell walked into the room. Campbell's face looked grim, and he was bone weary tired of all the game that was being run. "We have to release Shannon Davenport," he said to Lombardo.

Lombardo narrowed his eyes. This was not the way he had played out the scene in his mind. "The hell we do. Why?"

"Shonda Hunt is why. She's Davenport's alibi. She says he was with her. Smokey Cooke, the Dome's bartender, confirms Shannon was in the bar with Shonda. He left the bar with her. He also says he saw Shannon lend Michael his lighter the other night. The medical examiner has confirmed that the time of death is consistent with the time Shannon was in the bar. He didn't murder Michael Claybay."

Campbell took a seat across from Lombardo.

Lombardo smacked his hand on the desk. "There's no doubt, huh?" Deep inside he had known it was too easy, but he had ignored the feeling. Grudgingly he had to admit that somebody with Shannon's street smarts wouldn't make a mistake like that.

Besides, he wasn't a young thug; he didn't come from the same cloth as these kids. He was an old-school planner. He would try hard to get away with whatever he was going to do.

Campbell said, "They've all been checked out. They're clean. No records. No nothing. There is one thing we can prove."

Lombardo brightened. "What's that?"

"Adultery."

Lombardo frowned.

"Shonda Hunt works for Tawney Davenport. It looks like she's been giving Shannon more comfort than Tawney."

Lombardo whistled. "Our boy doesn't travel far for his sympathy. Still, he'll slip. When he does I'll be there because I'm his looking glass."

Campbell knew Lombardo wasn't letting this go. For some reason Shannon rubbed him the wrong way. Maybe because Shannon had pushed him in the hospital and gone down on him, breaking the legendary choke hold Lombardo had on him. He had to admit Shannon Davenport had moves on him.

He also knew it didn't help that Shannon kept addressing Lombardo as a cracker. It was pure nastiness on Shannon's part and definitely not helping with Lombardo's attitude.

Newark was one of the few pro-black cities in the country. Primarily it was run and controlled by blacks at least on the surface. There was a black mayor and a black city council. He knew a lot of blacks resented having white officers in their neighborhoods policing them. He guessed Shannon was of this breed.

Still, he was tired of all the piss-ass games on both sides of the fence. He was getting too old for this crap. He had become a police officer because he felt that his people needed their own heroes. That they needed to handle their own problems. But there were days when he felt he was fighting a losing battle. It seemed that for every one of them they got off the streets for distributing their poisons and violence, ten more popped up to take their place.

Ten more were anxious to prove themselves, to be in the know. They wanted to be invincible. If it wasn't that, then there were ten million black kids in the country wanting to be the next Michael Jordan. As if bouncing a basketball would be their savior. They never took the time to look at the odds.

Campbell thought about the three young brothers from Newark who had written that book called *The Pact*. They had struggled from these same neighborhoods, but they had beaten the odds and lived to tell about it. They had become doctors and dentists working in their own neighborhood.

They even had their own clinic. He wished more young black kids would read that book, be inspired, and follow that example.

Instead he felt like he was faced with a million to one who wanted to be top-dog criminals. What a thing to aspire to. They didn't want to look weak in front of their friends. So there was a constant cycle of proving one's self. And the game was getting deadlier and bloodier by the day.

Campbell sighed, picking up the phone. He punched a button. "Shannon Davenport is free to go."

A short while later Lombardo tapped on the bars of Shannon's cell. Shannon, who had been leaning back on his bunk, opened his eyes.

"Just remember. I'm your looking glass," Lombardo told Shannon with a gleam in his eye.

A police officer appeared behind Lombardo with the paperwork and keys.

Discovering the primary source of his release from the murder charge, later that day Shannon decided to thank Shonda for being stand-up. They stood outside on her front porch.

"You didn't have to help me," Shannon said. He looked out across the street thoughtfully. "I owe you."

Shonda put a soft hand to his cheek, looking deeply into his eyes. Shannon mistakenly believed the glow that peeked out from her eyes was warmth.

She looked up at him, adoringly and with a keen sense of want. "I did have to help you," she said softly.

"Why?"

"Because that's what friends are for," she whispered like a breeze in his ear.

It was a good thing Shannon never went into the house, because he would definitely have gotten an idea of what a breeze suddenly turned into a cyclone could do.

Nana Mama, who was peeking out from behind the curtain, observed the face her granddaughter was showing Shannon Davenport. It was trickery, nothing but pure trickery.

Trembling the old woman hurried back to her room as fast as her years would allow. Picking up the phone she punched in the number of the one woman she knew she could talk to.

Mama.

Chapter 21

When Ballistic had stated he wanted a fear deeper than the depths of hell to fall on Rico DeLeon Hudson, he had meant it. Literally.

So far Trey, Warren P., and Bobby had done a good job of taking down Rico's houses and tracking down his right-hand man, Eight Ball. Taking him out of his misery had been Ballistic's pleasure.

If he hadn't needed to give Eight Ball's head to Rico to make his point, it would have become a trophy to be hung up on the wall as one of his many accomplishments.

Milkbone's death was a bonus.

He happened to step out of Rico's Jeep at an opportune moment. He just wanted this little punk to know that he never slept. That he could be wherever he was, controlling the situations, slipping in and out, like a ghost in the night.

He had acknowledged Rico's little grandstand play at Spence's funeral. It was pure child's play. But Rico had mistakenly stepped over the boundaries. He had disrespected a bond, so for that he would have to pay dearly. And today was the day. Ballistic would take care of this personally. An eye for an eye.

Rico's cell phone was ringing off the hook because a number of his stash houses and street lieutenants had been hit. Some of them were minor players, but coldly and systematically Ballistic was spreading his web.

And Rico hadn't gotten the most important call of all yet. But he would.

The saying goes, as a man thinketh so is he, and Ballistic was a man with very dark thoughts. He was also a carrier. He carried out whatever came to his mind. It was all a game to him. It was a very dangerous one because Ballistic had no conscience. There was no stop mechanism in his brain, nothing that registered compassion or sympathy. No regrets for pain and sorrow.

He was like a machine covered in flesh. An open vessel for whatever evils spewed forth from the land. And he was loving his position. He had cheated death more times than he could remember. The testament was in the hole in his throat and the limp he walked with.

However, these weren't handicaps. They were badges of honor. He wore them as though they were prestigious. They were a salute to the Darkling. Evidence that he was a man who would pay what he owed, for receiving more than one life.

Ballistic was sometimes a man of two faces. Not both of them were his. He looked into the red eyes of his German shepherd. The unusual color mesmerized him.

He crossed his legs, diverting his attention from the dog, giving a full-force impact of his presence to Kesha, Rico's lady.

She was sitting in a chair across from him in Rico's living room. Ballistic acknowledged silently that the boy had taste in both living large and women. Kesha was a tasty-looking little morsel. However, her sensuality didn't faze him in the least. He had long ago lost any sexual appetite he might have had.

Sex was a weakness for most men. It had caused the downfall of many of them. Ballistic knew he would never be among such numbers. He had no desire for women other than what he could use them for. They were simply tools, a means to an end.

For a brief moment Ballistic got caught up in the reverie of his past. He had been sodomized repeatedly from the age of five to the age of thirteen by his mentally ill stepfather.

The man should have been institutionalized, but in the black community counseling, psychiatry, or anything that smacked of it was taboo. Doctors were for white people. Churches were for black people. Unfortunately neither antidote had been enlisted to help Ballistic, although his mother was a staunch Christian.

She was a Christian who never seemed to see the face of evil, though. Not in its purest form. Only now after so many losses was she beginning to recognize it. Even though she'd had recent cause to come in close contact with it, she would never fathom the magnitude of it that had burst forth from her own womb.

The deranged twisted systematic stripping away of Ballistic's sexuality stopped on his thirteenth birthday. That was the day Ballistic put a bullet in his stepfather's head and buried his body beneath the cellar, leaving his mother to raise two children on her own. She thought he had simply walked out and left her a single parent.

Ballistic left her with her thoughts. Doing so was easier than the truth. That had been his first body. After that he had sat over that grave in the dark on many a night summoning the powers of darkness, getting high as a kite. Two things had come from it. He never had a craving for women. And he had come upon a power to be reckoned with.

Ballistic pulled his thoughts back to the present.

Kesha shivered as a glow peeked out from the depths of Ballistic's coal-black eyes. She'd never seen such emptiness. There was no way she could appeal to this man.

She felt it deep in her bones. There was nothing to connect to. Sitting before her was not an ordinary thug or gangster, and she knew that, instinctively.

No. Although this man possessed the physicality of humankind, his spirit was not such. Kesha could feel waterfalls of sweat pouring from between her armpits.

She looked at the German shepherd, then back at Ballistic. With astonishment she saw that the pupils of both their eyes were red. Something dark clawed at her memory banks, but for the life of her she couldn't put her finger on it. So instead she shivered as though she had been thrown in a freezer.

She looked over at Bobby, Warren P., and Trey. Her eyes

pleaded with them to reconsider, to help her. Although they put up a good front, each one of them was as terrified of Ballistic as she was. They would be no help, she realized with a pang.

Looking back at Ballistic through his eyes she fast-forwarded through a tunnel, tons of dirt fell on her face and her body suffocating her. She tunneled through pure blackness. There was no light. Finally, he released her.

Kesha heaved trying to get air. As quickly as she had been transported through the tunnel of Ballistic's eyes, she found herself back, bound and gagged in the face of darkness. She had taken a mind trip into the depths of hell, seeing her own burial in the process.

He smiled. Kesha nodded, her heart hammering in her chest, knowing her death was sealed, and she had been given an opportunity to stare it in the face.

She was only glad her daughter wasn't there. Her sister was babysitting for Ebony. Thank God. She would be spared the same fate as her mother because Kesha knew if Ebony had been there for this monster, it would have made no difference. He would take whatever life was in the house.

Ballistic tilted his head just as Kesha raised hers a bit higher, her chin pointed in a position of pride. He felt his first stir of admiration as he realized she was facing her death without pleading, begging, sobbing, or crying. Respect tingled through his body. He'd seen men who didn't have her strength.

Then he nodded at the dog that had been awaiting his silent signal. In that moment Kesha knew what had been tingling at the base of her memory. She was staring at a man marked by the devil. The revelation broke out a new sheen of sweat on her skin. She didn't believe she'd ever been that close to evil until now.

In a flash she knew this was about more than hustling, gangbanging, clocking dollars, and wearing designer clothes. It was about more than the game they had all played. This was high stakes, and it was not on the grounds or by the rules with which they were used to playing.

In Ballistic's eyes she saw more than mere revenge. She saw

eyes that weren't his. She saw, simply put, damnation. And an eye for an eye.

"Lord Jesus," was all she said aloud, but in her heart she sent out a prayer for all of their very souls. She prayed for forgiveness in the last hour. They had been dancing with the devil and didn't even know it.

At Ballistic's nod the German shepherd attacked the bound Kesha. He sank his clawed teeth into her soft skin, tearing her to shreds. The girl's screams were quickly silenced as the dog tore her windpipe from her throat.

He shook her like a rag doll. Mercifully by this time Kesha's spirit had separated from her body so there was no more pain and terror. It was just as well she had been spared the sight of her own body being ripped to shreds, and gasoline being thrown in her face.

Quickly they doused the entire house with gasoline. On a look from Ballistic they lit the match torching the girl and the house.

Ballistic limped back out the way he had come. The only thing left was the Darkling, whose howls of anger reverberated in the intense burning flames of the house as he stared at the darkened, black charcoal carnage of the body on the floor.

As the spirit had separated from the body the Darkling had missed an opportunity to gather it as one of his own, and he was incensed with anger.

Unknowingly Ballistic silently saluted him, not knowing that in the flesh he had hit his mark, but in the spirit he had missed his shot.

The Darkling didn't accept misses.

Chapter 22

Mama watched as Aisha climbed from the car with her mother. Nikki, Aisha's mother, looked shell-shocked. She was a young mother. She had given birth to Aisha at the age of fifteen. She was neither equipped nor prepared for the fate that had befallen her daughter.

On the other hand Aisha's eyes shone bright with both fear and knowledge. Mama keyed in on it straightaway, although Nikki hadn't a clue. They had just come from the second round of doctor visits empty-handed. None of them were able to provide a clue as to why Aisha had suddenly lost her speech.

They were chalking it up to emotional and psychological. Asking all kinds of insane questions. To which Nikki had taken deep offense. Her daughter was not crazy. Neither was she for that matter.

That's why she never went to doctors. But she was so afraid for her daughter she had relented. She wished she hadn't, because they didn't seem to know a damn thing.

Knowing she was stressed out, Mama called out to Nikki from her front porch, "Nikki!"

Nikki turned at the sound of Mama's voice.

"Child, bring that baby over here to me," Mama yelled out to her. She wanted to see the child up close as well as find out if she might be able to get a moment alone with her.

Tears shimmered in Nikki's eyes as she did what Mama requested. When she reached the front steps of the porch Mama didn't waste any time. "What'd them there doctors say, Nikki?" she said while gathering Aisha close to her apron strings for a warm hug. The child was trembling. This angered Mama.

"Aw, you know, Mama, they said the same old thing. Bottom line is they just don't know. I'm gonna have to try to apply for some special schooling or something because she can't attend regular classes anymore. I don't have that kind of money."

Mama drew Aisha closer to her while she stared in Nikki's eyes. "Now, you hush your mouth about money, child. You're gonna have what you need. I got a few dollars put away for emergencies. This is one if I ever seen it. So you just find out what you need and let me know."

"No. Honestly, I couldn't—"

Mama cut Nikki off in midsentence. "You can and you will. I ain't fixing to take no for an answer. Now, why don't you go lie down and rest a bit? I'm going take Aisha inside with me, give her a slice of my lemon meringue pie, and she and I's going to spend some time together. Okay?"

Nikki nodded, grateful. She hugged Mama before leaving the porch. "You're a godsend. I'll come back for her in a little while."

Mama nodded. "God ain't sent all he's gone send yet, Nikki. You just remember that."

Although Nikki thought that an odd statement she only nodded. Everybody knew Mama wasn't like the rest of them. She never had been. She'd fed, babysat, and clothed more babies in their neighborhood than any of them could remember. And she'd always been prone to strange sayings.

Now she was coming to the rescue again with money. Nikki said a silent prayer for Mama and went into her house. Mama gathered up Aisha, taking her straight to her sitting room where she could get to the bottom of things.

Aisha loved Mama; she always had. Mama was sweet and warm,

and had always provided Aisha with all the things grandmothers were for. Aisha felt especially close to her because her own grandmother had died when she was younger. She had overdosed in a drug house.

The scars on her arms from Old King Heroin had been a testament to the pain living inside the woman. Her arms had been covered from top to bottom in tracks. There wasn't an inch of flesh that hadn't been scarred from the needle.

Although she was a junkie she had loved, as well as provided for and nurtured, her daughter and granddaughter. Her death had left a deep void in both Nikki's and Aisha's life that had never been filled.

Nikki stretched out on the couch in the living room after kicking off her shoes. She was exhausted. She had been a nervous wreck as well since she discovered that Aisha could no longer speak. She was asleep almost before her head hit the pillow.

Mama cut Aisha a nice slice of pie and sat down next to the child after pouring her some cold milk as well. This was going to be delicate because of Aisha's age. But she knew what Aisha had seen. She only needed to make her speak of it. She had to face it, so she could begin the healing process. That couldn't happen unless she overcame her fear.

Papa, who sat in the living room but could see into the sitting room, cut his eyes in Mama's direction. He'd told her not to meddle, but he'd known better. He'd been reading Scriptures on a nightly basis ever since Mama had uttered the words *rockabye, baby*.

He shut his eyes tightly against the shrieking, tormented cries of long ago. They were all running against the wind. The past had a way of catching up to folks. Now it was pronouncing its evil, holding this child in its clutches. And she wasn't the worst of it.

He knew Aisha was only meant to be a witness. The worst of it lay beyond his door being enacted out on the streets, penetrating the flesh. It was if he'd ever seen it, the active order of the principalities of darkness.

Mama placed a warm hand over Aisha's. Papa returned his attention to reading the *Star Ledger* newspaper. Better to let Mama do her work. Much as he didn't want to be involved, he knew there was no choice. That's why he was getting prayed up and reading his Scriptures.

Aisha bowed her head and stared at the lemon meringue pie, but she didn't touch it. She didn't acknowledge Mama's hand over hers either. Mama pursed her lips before speaking. "Aisha?"

The child didn't look up.

"Aisha, this here's Mama talking to you. Look at me, child."

The only response was the trembling of Aisha's hand. It had taken on a life of its own. It was shaking with the furor of a tidal wave. Mama's hand, which covered hers, was every bit as mobile.

Mama lifted Aisha's hand, trying to rub warmth into it. She willed stillness into the child's hand.

"Aisha. Baby, don't be afraid."

Aisha lifted her head as though by remote. That awful stench, the one that had plagued her since she saw the Darkling, reached her nostrils. The name of the thing just popped into her head out of nowhere. *The Darkling*. There it was.

Now she knew the thing was called the Darkling. She could also sense that it had female traits, as well as male traits, but she didn't know how she knew that.

She also knew Mama couldn't smell the stink of it and she couldn't even ask her. She wrinkled her nose. It was like rotting eggs that had been hidden for a long time. She convulsed and threw her head back in the air.

"Oh no, you don't, demon." Mama was on her feet. "In the name of Jesus the Nazarene, she ain't one of yours."

Quickly Mama retrieved her bottle of holy olive oil, splashed a cross over Aisha's forehead, and spoke once more. "In the mighty name of Jesus, not this child."

Aisha's head righted. Her body stopped convulsing. She looked at Mama scared, confused. Mama dabbed at the bit of spittle that was forming at the child's mouth with her apron string.

"It's all right, baby. It's all gonna be all right. Mama's here."

Aisha sniffed the air. The foul stench was gone. With a steady hand she covered Mama's hand with her own for a brief moment. Then she reached for her fork, sticking it into her slice of pie.

"When the Lord is ready for you to speak to his glory, Aisha, you will. Jesus is there for you, baby." Mama now knew with a certainty there would be no forcing this child to speak. It was not on their time.

Aisha nodded. She didn't feel as scared as she did before. When Mama had said Jesus' name and made the sign of the cross on her forehead the bad smell had gone away. In that moment Aisha had known two things. One was the power of Jesus Christ. Two was the fact that she would one day speak again when it was time.

She took a sip of her milk, smiling at Mama. Papa had given up all pretense of reading his paper a while ago. He traded looks with Mama over the child's head.

Chapter 23

Mama had barely returned Aisha to Nikki when a sight for her old tired eyes pulled up at the curb of her house. Painstakingly slow, one arthritic leg took hold on the sidewalk as Shonda's nana mama climbed slowly from the taxi.

Although she and Mama spoke frequently by phone, it had actually been a few years since they'd had a visit in person.

Nana Mama, as she was known by her oldest living friends, what few there were left, that is, smiled at Mama. The taxi driver helped her onto the sidewalk. She paid her fare, then hobbled on down the walkway up to Mama's house on her cane.

When she finally reached the porch Mama just grabbed her and hugged her. Papa smiled from his place on the couch at the sight of Nana Mama. She was one of the truest people he had ever known.

Besides, there weren't too many of them left. Certainly there weren't many of them that had been there on that night. On reflection with startling realization Papa became aware it was just the three of them left—Nana Mama, Mama, and him. All the others were already dead.

Being the gentleman he was, Papa rose from his seat upon Nana Mama's entry into the living room.

She smiled. "Aren't you a sight for sore eyes?" She beamed.

Papa was dressed to the nines as usual with a razor-sharp crease in his trousers and matching suspenders on his crisp blue shirt. In his day he had been one dapper man.

Papa had been as sharp as a tack and as handsome as the day was long. There was many a teary eye when Mama snagged him. But what God put together let no man put asunder, for Mama and Papa were going nigh on sixty years of courtship and marriage, and it was obvious they still loved one another as much as the first time they'd met.

They were childhood sweethearts. They had grown up together as children. You could see the sparkle and spark strong as ever when they looked at each other. Their friendship and love had held tight throughout the time.

Nana Mama sat down with Mama's assistance in the rocking chair. "George," she said, addressing Papa by his given name, "you gone on and sit down now."

Papa smiled. He grabbed the crease in his trousers, while sitting down. It was a gesture of old.

Mama took her place. She was about to speak when she scrunched up her eyes in pure aggravation. One of Nana Mama's eyes was black and blue. In fact her skin had dark patches of blue black in varying degrees, along with purple splotches covering her skin.

She could also see the red welt marks around her neck. On closer inspection Mama noticed that she was much frailer than the last time she'd seen her, and she didn't think it was just age. Fury welled up in Mama's bosom.

Papa was following Mama's train of thought. Sometimes that happened even when they didn't speak to each other. He reared back in his seat as the word *abuse* took its place in his mind.

Mama came straight to the point. "Nana Mama, what's going on?" She shut her eyes. "Please don't tell me what I think."

Nana Mama cast her eyes downward in shame. She didn't want to burden her friends with her pain and all, but she had nowhere to turn. She couldn't take much more of the fierce beatings Shonda was giving her and still survive. Not to mention the emotional drain. And she desperately needed somebody to talk to.

"That girl's been beating you?"

Nana Mama nodded.

Papa shook his head.

"Aw, Nana Mama, that child is the devil's ware. I never thought I'd see the day," Mama huffed.

Nana Mama was quiet.

"Well, so be it." Mama pointed her finger. "But whatever beating you done took is to be the last one, and I mean that on my dead mama's grave."

Tears sprang to Nana Mama's eyes. Papa knew her pain would come to an end, because his Mama was always swift to action. He heard the determination in her voice and knew they would do whatever needed to be done to help Nana Mama.

He smiled reassuringly. "Mama's right, Nana Mama can't go on. You know that."

She nodded. "Yeah. But it's not such an easy pill to swallow. That child is flesh of my flesh. We ain't supposed to abandon our own flesh."

"Nana Mama, cut that out," Mama said. "You know once the devil gets in between something, that don't hold no water. Jesus said you either gathering with me or against me, ain't no middle ground."

"Hmmph," was all that came from Papa.

Nana Mama sighed. "That's what he said all right. He counted those people as his family as those that were doing the will of his heavenly father, not by blood but by spirit. I knows that. Don't make it no easier, though. Although Lord knows I look in that child's eyes and what I see makes my blood run cold."

"As the kids say, Nana Mama, this is out a' order. But your situation ain't all that's out a' order. There's some spirits around here that's out a' order too that need to be cast back, so it's just as well you're here. And here's where you'll stay. It's only me, you, and Papa left and we gone need to put our heads together."

"What you talking about, Pearline?" Nana Mama said, her mind suddenly cast away from her problems. Her spine was tingling from the tone in Mama's voice.

"You member that night long ago?" Mama said.

Nana Mama rolled her eyes. "I ain't likely to forget."

"Good. 'Cause just as it was sworn, it's back."

Nana Mama's eyes got big as saucers. Her expression near 'bout reflected the same exact expression on Papa's face. "They say the hand that rocks the cradle rules the world, Pearline."

"In this world, Nana Mama, that hand has got to be cut off. Might have to be us doing some of the cutting."

At that moment a deep black howling emitted from the fireplace. All three of them turned to look in unison. Goose bumps sprouted on their arms.

If they could have read each other's minds they would have found that they were all having the same thought. They all wished once upon a time that they had not seen what they'd seen. But they had and now it was time to pay the piper.

Chapter 24

In the conference room at the bank Tawney sat at the head of a long, polished, gleaming cherry-wood table in the midst of the plush, comfortably designed room filled with green plants.

It had been one of the many ideas she'd had implemented. She believed that if you surrounded people in an atmosphere they enjoyed being in and derived pleasure from that you would motivate them to their highest performance by virtue of subliminal messaging so to speak.

Since she was one heck of a performer for the bank they had obliged her idea. Tawney could outwork any number of her staff put together. The management was in awe of the way she turned projects around, although the actual level of their awe was mostly kept to themselves.

Still, she carried weight in the bank, and people knew it. She was one of the very few African-Americans who did carry such weight, and she did so with the utmost respect.

Tawney at thirty-three was class with a capital C. Her breeding and style were impeccable. The only blight on her seemingly intellectual, stylistic life was the thug she had married.

Instead of being out in the upscale South Orange where she belonged and could afford to be she was slumming in Newark.

Catering to Shannon's whims about staying with his people. Exasperating.

And she was not in just any part of Newark. She was in the Central Ward, which was known for being the most dangerous part of Newark. You couldn't walk the streets at certain times of the night. Recently a fifteen-year-old boy had been jacked for his bike and killed.

It was monstrous.

Shannon could have at least moved her into the Ironbound section of Newark. Ferry Street was known for its cuisine. There were restaurants galore. Some of them had been written up in food reviews, such was their reputation. She'd also bet her bottom dollar that Ironbound didn't have the security issues of the Central Ward.

Ironbound was primarily Portuguese and Brazilian. They had built commerce in that tiny patch of dirt in Newark, creating a community all their own, so there was no way they would be plagued with the problems or blights the Central Ward of Newark carried. They weren't having it.

At the time in her life that she'd met Shannon, South Orange, and Ironbound were far from her mind. She hadn't cared what patch of dirt she lived on as long as she had Shannon.

Girlfriend had hungered after the magnetic dark sensual looks of Shannon Davenport, who was four years her senior. Her hunger for him was intense. The sound of his voice mesmerized her.

The weight of a look from the man was more than she could bear. He'd had a smile to die for. Charm oozed every time he looked at her. Every time he smiled. And he had a pair of the most beautiful translucent brown eyes that she'd ever seen.

She used to get butterflies and a tightening in her stomach, just looking at him. Shannon Davenport was a man's man in every sense of the word. Having him would be on his own terms. He wasn't accustomed to taking orders, or bending. She knew that.

He was rugged, rough, tough, and streetwise with a hint of arrogance. Respect was his middle name. The sound of his name inspired awe as well as fear in the streets. He was nigga rich and confident.

Most intriguing of all he knew how to treat a lady. And although his persona from head to toe had screamed *thug,* for her he had the soul of an angel.

She would've thought one of the street princesses, a woman of his own caliber, would have wound up with him. Enough of them were throwing themselves at him, that was for sure. But he wanted her.

The rest was history.

He was everything that she was not. When she fell she fell hard. The walls came tumbling down.

When Jazz was born the neighborhood bothered her a bit, but she kept trying to appease Shannon. She'd spent tons of money on the inside of the house to make up for the neighborhood. Her house was nothing more than a ghetto palace.

She told herself that Jazz was small and that before she reached the critical age, they would move. It never happened.

Now she was paying her dues for loving and living beneath her own status. Too late she had found out how dangerous it was to live beneath your means. It had cost her more than she was able to pay. Maybe the naysayers had been right. She should have married a doctor or a lawyer.

She heard her own voice of conscience. "But then there would have been no Jazz. Would there be, Tawney?"

What difference did it make if there'd never been Jazz? There still wasn't Jazz now. Tawney swallowed hard to keep from crying.

Jazz had been so very much like Shannon. He had been the best father. Fatherhood fit him like a second glove. His daughter was his world. He'd treated her like a princess.

Shaking herself out of her reverie, facing the unpleasant task before her, Tawney cleared her throat and returned to addressing her staff. "To sum this up, the incidents of unprofessional behavior on the floor must stop. If you have problems you cannot resolve with a coworker, see me. And please watch your performance times. The new budget is in full effect, and senior management is keeping a close eye. Any questions?"

One of Tawney's staff members spoke up. "Yeah."

"Yes, Debbie?"

"Will there be any loss of jobs? I need my job."

Immediately there was a chorus of agreement and head shaking going on.

"As long as we live within the current budget, there will not be. This isn't a downsize."

The expressions around the cherry-wood table were disbelieving. Shonda rolled her eyes. She leaned over to the woman next to her, saying, "I've heard that before."

Tawney stared at Shonda. "Shonda, do you have something you want to share with the rest of us?"

Shonda did a quick retreat. "No, Tawney. I'm all set."

Tawney closed her portfolio, folding her hands on top of it. "I've shared the information that I have at this time. Is there anything else?"

The staff was quiet.

"That's it, then. Make sure you record one hour for the meeting."

They filed from the room. As soon as they were in the hallway out of earshot Shonda pulled Debbie and Beverly away from the crowd. "Let's go outside and smoke a cigarette."

Outside the bank the women lit their cigarettes. Debbie looked at Shonda. "So, Shonda, what's up?"

Shonda blew a smoke ring. "Tawney is what's up. She makes me sick." Shonda's voice dripped hatred like a fungus. "She's always fronting."

"Fronting about what, Shonda?"

Shonda looked around, making sure the only ones in earshot were the ones she wanted. "You know, she acts like she's all that. Ms. Professional. But I know niggas who used to serve her back in the day."

Debbie and Beverly exchanged glances. "Serve her what, Shonda?" Debbie said.

Shonda sneered. "Don't be so damned naive, Debbie."

Debbie took a step back in surprise at Shonda's tone and choice of words.

"Seriously. Naiveté doesn't suit you. Cocaine, that's what."

Beverly shook her head. Ms. Shonda was a dangerous diva. "How do you know that?"

Shonda walked away from the building. She puffed on her cigarette. The two of them followed. "I know, that's all."

Turning to face them, venom slicing her every word, she said, "She thinks she's all that. But she's married to an Original O.G. I bet she don't want the boys on the second floor to know about that. You know, them senior managers that sign her paycheck.

"Her husband, Shannon Davenport, is a damned gangster. That nigga was huge back in the day. Now that whore is trying to play it out like he's retired or something. She ain't fooling anybody."

Debbie was not feeling Shonda. She didn't know why it was that black women had to throw stones at the ones who were trying to step up the ladder. It was the same old "crabs in a barrel" syndrome. She was sick of it.

She was also sick of the lethal, poisoned tongued Shonda, so she said, "I don't know about her background, but the girl is good at what she does. She worked hard in this bank to get where she is. I know because I saw her. And most of the time I think she tries to play it fair."

Shonda tossed her blond-weaved braids arrogantly. A glint of something Debbie didn't recognize peeked out from her eyes. "Think what you like. What you think and what it is are two different things."

Beverly, who had been playing with a lock of her hair during the exchange, stepped in. She had always been a come-straight-to-the-point person, and the arrogant lethal Shonda didn't stop her now. "If you feel all like that, then why are you always up in her face?"

Shonda stubbed out her cigarette with a major attitude. She bit her tongue. Anger welled up inside her like thunder building.

It was all she could do not to smack this smart-mouthed heifer to the ground. However, she knew it wouldn't be the thing to do just yet. Even though Beverly was the one who kicked off her anger, all she could think was Tawney would get hers when the time came.

Trying to get a grip she said sweetly, "She's the boss. A girl's got to do what a girl's got to do. I'll have what she's got. Soon. Real soon."

Disgust rose up simultaneously in their eyes.

Shonda rolled her eyes. "I don't know why you're looking at me like that. You probably feel the same way and just don't have the nerve to say it. Especially with Tawney, who can flip back and forth between the hood and corporate America like the flick of a light switch."

Shonda turned on them, switching her hips, walking toward the building. Over her shoulder she said, "It ain't over till it's over, girlfriends."

Chapter 25

Shannon Davenport sat in the midst of forces that he couldn't begin to imagine. He had trouble with the police, trouble with the gangs, a wife who hated him, and a daughter who was lost to him, as well as a young street punk who was out to kill him and make a name for himself.

Yeah. He knew Rico DeLeon Hudson was trying to represent as well. Old school versus new school. Take out an original gangster and seal the pact. Solidify. Niggas young and old having to give you the props. By taking him out Rico would put fear in the old-timers. There was already a lack of respect. He knew how Rico was trying to roll.

That fear would earn him respect as well as money. Too many old-timers now were talking about how you couldn't mess with them young boys. That was a serious mistake because now these young punks were walking around with their chests poked out, with automatic weapons, and a serious disregard for life.

Shannon knew the game. He had once been Rico DeLeon Hudson. But he wasn't now and that was the major difference.

All this represented what Shannon knew. What he didn't know and couldn't fathom was the trouble brewing around him, which wasn't attached to or dressed in flesh. Yeah, it was all coming down to more than just street wars. There were dues to be paid.

At the very moment that he sat in Je's Soul Food Restaurant at the corner of William and Halsey streets in downtown Newark, there was another entity entering the mix.

Actually it had already entered. The forces were aligning, placing Shannon Davenport in their orbit. This was far from good. In the mix were blackness, hatred, demented souls, and failed promises.

The waitress set the steaming plate of smoked ham, grits, cheese eggs, and biscuits in front of him along with a steaming cup of coffee.

Shannon felt better already. Once he had eaten he could decide his next course of action. Je's was just what he needed to add a feeling of normalcy to his life. The restaurant had been in Newark a good many years.

It was a popular spot among Newark's residents. The food was warm, homey, and cooked to perfection. Some of the waitresses had been there for as long as he could remember. It was almost like being among family.

He glanced up at a picture of Martin Luther King, who seemed to be presiding over or perhaps residing in the midst of all the madness. Lord knew he was a man who had lived and died in the midst of chaos.

Now the people he had fought so hard for were dying on the streets named after him. He was probably rolling over in his grave at the tragedy of it.

Shannon stared at him for a moment longer, feeling the kinship, seeing the cross. Remembering another man who had paid the ultimate price being nailed to that cross.

King had been a man who'd wanted to be among his people as well. What was so wrong with that? Jesus had been a man who walked among them, wanted to give them salvation and free them. What was so wrong with that?

He glanced around at the rest of the walls, which were full of various African art. Better not to start down that road of thinking. In fact the thought of Jesus surprised him a bit. He'd always been a believer; he just wasn't mushy about it.

Maybe Jazz's death was causing him to reconsider a great many things. He'd been thinking about the Lord a lot since she'd died. He shook his head, disgusted. He was typically black. When the trouble came down he looked up.

Otherwise he never looked in that direction. His child's death was making him do so now.

Glancing out the window he saw a woman dressed from head to toe in black silk. That in itself wasn't strange. What was strange was the fact that a solid black veil covered her entire face.

You could tell it was a female by the way it moved. How the hell could she see where she was going?

She was pushing a shopping cart filled to the brim with garbage. She stopped. Turned. Appeared to stare directly at Shannon. Though how that could be was impossible since her face was covered.

Shannon felt a surge of energy flow through his body. He looked, blinked, and found himself staring at the braiding salon that was across the street.

There was no sign of any woman with a black veil covering her face or dressed entirely in black.

For some reason he felt spooked, but he shook himself out of it, returning to his thoughts. It was just as well. Flying over the rooftop of Je's was a black-winged creature whose beak poked through the solid black veil, and whose wings ripped through the black silk.

It was a sign of things to come.

At one time in Je's there'd been a piano perched over in the corner near the small bar. On Sunday mornings you could listen to gospel along with your breakfast or just some mellow tunes on the ivory if you went through Je's on the right evening.

He used to bring Tawney there all the time. They would gorge themselves with terrific heart-of-the-South soul food, sit holding hands, staring in each other's eyes as the music played.

Shannon shook his head. It all seemed so long ago. That was before Jazz was born. Now Jazz had been born and had both lived as well as died. Guilt for keeping his family in Newark was eating him alive.

Even though they had the money he hadn't wanted to be one

of the ones who ran out to the suburbs abandoning the neighborhood home front. He was comfortable where he was.

Besides, that would've been Tawney's thing, not his. He didn't have the kind of mentality that went with perfectly manicured lawns, Seton Hall University, and Saks Fifth Avenue charge cards. Tawney had been right when she accused him of not wanting to leave. The suburbs weren't his scene.

But what was? He didn't know. All he knew was the streets he called home had swallowed up his only child alive and he was having a hard time living with that. He'd wanted his daughter to know where she came from. He'd wanted her to be successful but real. Now he didn't have a daughter. The streets had stolen her life from him.

If he were honest with himself he'd have to admit the one sore point for him with his wife was the fact that she wanted to leave. He resented her for that. He felt people should hold their own. If there was a problem do something about it. Make it better.

Now that he'd lost Jazz he wasn't so sure he was right about staying. Maybe Tawney was right. Maybe if he'd done it her way Jazz would still be alive. That thought pierced the core of his heart.

That single thought that his stubbornness might have cost him his daughter was more than he could bear. She had been the one thing in the entire world that he truly loved.

He pushed the plate away, signaling the waitress for the check. The food suddenly tasted like lead in his mouth.

It was time to formulate a plan. But first he needed to go home. He would do that under the cover of darkness. Tonight.

Chapter 26

Back in the warehouse when they were alone Trey took a chance on breaking the "no speaking until you're spoken to" rule and said to Ballistic, "Rico got what he deserved. Though it could be considered a waste of some nice-looking flesh."

He smiled, trying to lightly joke with Ballistic. Ballistic stared at him piercingly.

He didn't even crack a smile.

Nervously Trey continued, "Rico dishonored Spence's mother. That nigga done lost his mind removing the body from the services. If that don't top it all, man. That nigga loves to grandstand. Spence's body was dumped in Branch Brook Park scattered with bullet holes. It looks like Swiss cheese."

Ballistic finally smiled.

He decided in this instance to let Trey go for speaking before he was spoken to. "That's why Rico's little piece is up in flames. Our boy has guts and imagination. No doubt."

Ballistic rapped his cane on the pole. The German shepherd stood attentive at his side. "Did you get what I asked for?"

Trey smiled. He reached inside his jacket, pulling out a stolen sports jersey belonging to Rico. He tossed it to Ballistic.

For his part he was glad Ballistic was in a good mood because he had learned that Ballistic was one foul nigga. Trey had never come up against anyone like him, and he hoped he never did again.

This nigga wasn't ordinary. He was on some extraordinary extra extra that none of the rest of them could touch.

Trey had never seen a man whose soul was as black as Ballistic's. It didn't have anything to do with game or just being straight-up jack.

This scared him in a place inside he didn't know existed. He wondered if the others felt it. He didn't know but even if they did, none of them would ever breathe a word of it. It just couldn't be done.

Trey was living with the feeling that they had seriously messed up in this life associating with Ballistic, and after this they all had hell to look forward to. But he was draped in the thug persona. Being stand-up, he could do nothing but play it to the bone.

Deep inside where a playa's bone resided he knew it was just a matter of time. That none of them would make it out. And for the first time in his life he knew it wasn't worth it, but he was stuck. He couldn't walk away and he could never let on that he felt this way.

His death would be sealed in short order if he did. There was no way out. That was the way of the hood. It swallowed and ate its own young.

Mentally Trey crossed himself.

Just in case this dude Jesus was real he was wondering if maybe he'd forgive him if he asked, for associating with a demon. 'Cause there was no doubt that the waves of darkness emanating from Ballistic had nothing to do with hustling.

He himself was just trying to clock a dollar and make himself a rep. He'd become a rock on the streets to keep niggas off him. On the streets you were as good as your connections. Ballistic's name alone would make niggas wet their pants, so being down with him had its bennies. But they were in over their heads and he knew it.

He'd heard that strange noise as they left Rico's girl in the burning house. It was an eerie howling that sounded like it came from another realm. A shrieking. Just like something out of the damned *Exorcist*. No joke.

He'd told his grandmama to stop preaching at him, but she didn't listen. That's how he knew about Jesus. His grandmama claimed Jesus could save anybody. He hadn't saved anyone Trey had known. Except his grandmama. But still . . .

If he died here maybe he could have a chance somewhere else. As soon as the thought crossed his mind he shook his head, remembering the desperate look in Rico's girl's eyes when she realized she was at the mercy of a monster and how there was nothing he would do to help her.

Her screams would be something he would live with night and day. They had cold-bloodedly killed the woman, and he had been a willing participant. Self-preservation. Fear.

If he had stepped in Ballistic would have killed him instantly. He had had no choice. Still, the hatred along with the self-loathing persisted. It persisted because he knew he was too weak to do anything except go on and on playing it to the bone.

He would play until the music stopped.

And one day he knew the music would stop. The last melody would definitely play and the only thing left would be death. He was nothing more than a killing machine and he knew those who killed would eventually be killed.

That was the bottom line.

Ballistic put Rico's jersey up to the dog's nose, letting him sniff, smell, and savor Rico's scent. He nodded and the dog tore the jersey to shreds.

Trey nodded at the jersey. "Temaine came through with the goods," he said.

A gurgling sound emitted from Ballistic's throat. "Temaine's a good man. I will have to get him out of Rico's camp soon. Send Rico some flowers for me. Do not kill him. He is mine. Understood?"

Trey nodded. "What about Shannon Davenport?"

"He is not in my way. Leave him. In fact I consider him useful. He serves my purposes well."

For some reason Trey's skin crawled at Ballistic's words.

Ballistic raised an eyebrow wondering why Trey was still standing there. Trey nodded while moving out of his sphere.

Proverbs: 1:16 For their feet run to evil, and make haste to shed blood.

Chapter 27

Rico was one incensed nigga. His cell phone had been blowing up as his stash houses, lieutenants, and street soldiers were being taken down. A number of them had caught body bags.

He had taught them well, but it was as though he had been caught with his pants down and he knew doggone well his pants weren't down. Nevertheless he felt like some schoolboy who had been caught off guard.

Ballistic wasn't to be taken lightly. He needed to kill this dude. Homes need to be M.I.A., missing in action. It needed to be quick because he was tampering with Rico's rep. His connect was getting jittery, blowing up his cell every time he heard about another takedown.

He couldn't make these Cubans understand, because they didn't speak his language. The only language they understood was m-o-n-e-y.

Liquid cash.

They weren't trying to hear anything else. If their cash was jeopardized, you were a dead man, and they moved on to more lucrative territory.

They obviously spoke the language of the hood, though, because they were plugged into trouble with their dope almost before it occurred. Rico found this curious, but this wasn't the time for him to mull it over and figure it out.

He'd finally turned his cell phone off as well as his various pagers because this crap was out of control. He understood Ballistic wasn't happy with his stance at the church, but it was what it was.

His job in life was to make that nigga miserable and then dead. Anybody in the game would know not to front on him. He wasn't taking no shorts.

This was only the beginning because he could see how homes played now. Ballistic played for keeps, plain and simple.

Silence overtook him for a moment as he tried to think. He and Temaine walked together in silence, finally rolling up on his Jeep. It was covered in flowers. The inside was full of them. The heavy perfumed smell of flowers was in the air everywhere.

A creepy feeling like someone walking over your grave shot through Rico's body.

"What the hell?" Temaine said.

But Rico couldn't respond. A chalk outline had been drawn around the Jeep. In blazing white chalk on the outside of the outline were the words: RIP KESHA!

"No," was all Rico could get out. On the tail end of that word the Jeep exploded. Rico and Temaine ducked for cover as debris flew all over the place.

Temaine smiled. Ballistic was one badass nigga. The man had style if he'd ever seen it. He couldn't wait to get down with that nigga.

Rico rolled up next to Temaine. "We've got to get to my house, man."

"Okay, let's do this."

Upon arriving on his street Rico knew he had yet to face his greatest loss. It was deep in his gut. In fact it had been there all day, but he was stand-up so he'd ignored it.

He'd turned his cell phone off after it kept blowing up with bad news, so he hadn't received the worst news of all. He'd disconnected himself from the tragedies of his people while trying to formulate a plan and lie low.

At least he was disconnected until he saw the RIP KESHA in a chalk outline and his Jeep blew up. His baby's mother. She was dead. He had as good as killed her himself.

He was so busy playing cat-and-mouse with Ballistic as well as watching and putting fear in Shannon Davenport that he hadn't put any cover on her.

He'd thought the rules of the game prevented her from being touched. She was off-limits according to the rules. That was the truth. Apparently the street code rules didn't apply here.

They hadn't applied to little Jasmine Davenport either. But he'd made good on that. A quick phone call had verified Ebony was alive and well with Kesha's sister. Bless Kesha for taking the baby there or Rico knew she would be dead too.

He wouldn't make the same mistake twice. He'd already made arrangements for Ebony to be moved immediately out of Jersey. These death-struck punks were killing anybody who was in their way. Death had knocked at his door and claimed one of his own.

Rico's street was filled with emergency vehicles. Fire trucks, police cars, an ambulance, and an assortment of recognizable as well as undercover police vehicles.

Temaine stood silently by his side. Rico didn't dare even attempt to approach his house, or rather the pile of ashes that was left of it, because the cops would definitely pick him up.

From what he could see, there were only ashes where the house had stood. He could see the still smoldering flames. He smelled the black soot of the fire along with the awful smell of burnt flesh. The smoke seared his eyes even at this distance.

The entire street was in hysterics and filled with blazing red, white, and blue flashing lights. Instinctively he knew there was nothing left of his fine Kesha but ashes. Ballistic wouldn't have left him a body. When he took a man down he took his all.

He stood in the shadows of dying flames, embers, and the passing of life, watching. He wanted to drop to his knees in agony. He wanted to rage, yell, just let out his pain. But he couldn't let the traitor Temaine see that. He'd learned to keep your friends close, but keep your enemies closer.

He wanted to drop down just to say a prayer at Kesha's passing, but he definitely couldn't let a nigga see that either. His girl was gone and he couldn't even pay a respect to her. He had to let her go as though she'd never existed. As though they'd never shared a life or formed one together.

So all he could do was stand, stare, and contemplate, while planning to kill Ballistic in the worst way possible. He felt for his daughter because she had just lost both parents at once. He wouldn't be around because he was definitely going to kill this nigga.

His death would be by torture. Nothing else would do. Rico turned on his cell. The moment he did it lit up.

"You have my deepest sympathies, baby boy," Ballistic gurgled in his ear. "By now I'm sure you can see there are no rules, Rico DeLeon Hudson."

Rico didn't speak because he couldn't.

Hovering in the smoke above where his house had stood was an image of something, black, possibly male or female. It looked like it was made out of the soot of the ashes. Where the whites of the eyes should have been was a deep mustard yellow. The pupils flashed red. This thing. *Oh my God!* The thing had wings. Its mouth was thrown open, emitting a Gallic cry. A loud shriek rent the air.

"Rockabye, baby," it shrieked.

Rico turned to see if Temaine saw what he saw, heard what he'd heard. However, it was obvious that Temaine didn't see or hear a thing.

A loud click in his ear ended Ballistic's call.

Chapter 28

That night Shannon walked down the street toward his house. He looked up in the sky to see a full moon. There he went, looking up again. As though the answer to his problems might be written there.

For no reason at all he shivered. The very air around him was alive. He had an audience, though it was yet unseen. The forces had been sowing seeds of hatred against him.

Between the realms of the natural and the supernatural the spirits were weighing in as though watching a prizefight. The principalities of darkness, as Papa had observed, were aligning themselves.

It was spiritual wickedness in high places.

It was more powerful than flesh, though many didn't believe that. It didn't matter. They would all be believers before it was all over. They took life too simply. Never bothering to look beyond that which they could see, feel, or touch.

Well, there were things that couldn't be seen with the natural eye. But like air, that didn't mean they weren't there.

The Darkling had no respect of persons. All it wanted was payback. Revenge. If you took, then you would be taken. These were the laws of the universe. Laws written before the advent of mere men.

Ah, the Darkling was a rainmaker. When it rained it would pour. Blood would be running in the streets. Souls would be lost. This was child's play. For now it would watch the mortals play themselves out, follow the pattern that had been prepared for their destruction.

After all, the Darkling had been created out of their destruction, out of their lustful, deceitful, and vengeful ways. And it would exact retribution in its own time.

Shannon stopped in his tracks. T-Bone stepped out in front of him, blocking his path. A crew of gangbangers stepped up immediately behind T-Bone.

Shannon looked shrewdly at him. He didn't twitch a muscle. "You're blocking my way. Move."

"Do you know who I am, partner?"

"No."

T-bone stepped closer. "Well, you should. You spilled some of my blood."

Shannon looked on the ground. Like a river raging he saw an illusion of some more of this punk's blood flowing down the street. Instead of feeding into that he said, "Look, man, you tell Rico if he wants some of me to come on. I'm tired of playing games with him."

"Rico will take care of you in his own good time. This ain't about Rico." With that T-Bone shoved Shannon backward.

Shannon was bugging. He just knew this young punk didn't put his hands on him. He shoved T-Bone clean off his feet. He planted his feet solidly on the sidewalk prepared to throw deathblows.

T-Bone slowly climbed to his feet. "This is about my brother, Michael Claybay."

Shannon hit T-Bone so hard it rocked his entire world. A few of his teeth flew right out of his mouth. Scrambling to his feet he came at Shannon again. Shannon kneed him in the chin, and then did a couple of body blows to his midsection. He wasn't even winded. T-Bone stumbled around, blood spurting, trying to gather himself, trying to focus.

The gang members, seeing that T-Bone was no match for Shannon, all jumped him at the same time. This dude was an O.G. street fighting was his game. They knew they would all have had trouble taking him on, on a one-on-one basis. So it was time for the proverbial beat-down.

Shannon threw blow after blow, but there were too many of them. In the process he broke some jaws and dislodged some more teeth, he heard a couple of bones crack, but there was no way he could win this fight.

They beat the daylights out of him until his blood was running in the streets. Then they ran leaving him bleeding on the sidewalk.

Shannon got up. Though he was badly bruised he made it to his house. Amazingly his pride was more injured than he was.

He had grown up in an era where in order to be a serious contender for street fighting you had to be able to take as good as you could give. He had always been able to take a lot of punishment as well as dish it out.

Walking into his living room he saw that his house was trashed. Someone had seriously wrecked the place. The stuffing had been cut out of the sofa. Chairs were broken and thrown around the room.

Black spray paint was everywhere. The aquarium had been turned over. Water was all over the wall-to-wall carpeting. It was soaked through and through. Glass and dead fish were scattered all over the rug.

The birdcage with the parrot in it was on the floor. Shannon walked over to the birdcage. He stooped down. The bird was lying in the cage with his throat cut. "Poor Pete," he muttered. Pete had been silenced.

An eerie shrieking sound rent through the dark of the night surrounding Shannon's house. The female-male-thing spread its wings across the dark of the sky just above Shannon's house. Another shiver raced through his body.

In her bedroom Aisha heard the shrieking of the Darkling. She shivered at the same time as Shannon Davenport. Being unable to speak she raced to her small desk in the room. On a pad in red marker she scribbled one word over and over again in her shaking hand. JESUS. JESUS. JESUS.

As she did so Mama looked up in her living room frowning. Papa lowered his paper and even Nana Mama from her spot in the guest bedroom in Mama's house strained her ears wondering if she had heard what she'd heard.

Shannon looked to the wall in the dining room. The artist had decided to switch from black spray paint to red. Apparently the artist wanted to give him a taste of creativity with their next message. Written on the dining room wall were the words YOU'RE NEXT.

Chapter 29

Shannon heard a noise behind him. He whirled around to see Tawney walk in. She stopped in pure horror at the sight that lay before her. Her mouth flew open but nothing came out. She backed her way to the door she had just walked through, her eyes wide with fright.

Something inside Tawney snapped. She couldn't believe her own eyes. Who would do something like this to her house? Who killed her daughter? Who shot up her house? Why? *Oh God! Oh God!* "Oh my God! Why?"

She felt the frame of the door against her back. All she could think of was getting away. Putting some distance between herself and the impending nightmare her life was becoming.

She exhaled and then leaped down the porch steps.

"Tawney!" Shannon yelled, shocked by her action. "Tawney!"

She didn't even heed the sound of his voice. She just knew she had to keep leaping. She had to get away. She needed some distance. Shannon ran out the door and leaped down the steps behind her.

Tawney sprinted down the street as though she were a prized horse on a racetrack. She was tall with long slender legs, and she had rhythm. She moved like a newborn colt. Shannon had never known she could run so fast.

"Tawney, stop. Where the hell are you going? Tawney! Tawney!"

She continued to run as though the devil himself were pursuing her. Shannon finally got close enough to tackle her. He landed on top of her. Both of them tumbled onto the hard concrete of the street.

Tawney fought wildly. Her fear turned into pure adrenaline, and she fought Shannon like a wildcat. She kicked and screamed, throwing him a right cross that caught him square on the jaw.

Finally Shannon pinned her hands down to her side. In a single stroke all the fight left Tawney. She hyperventilated, sobbing. Tears ran down her face.

Shannon grabbed her to him. He held her against his chest. "I'm sorry, baby. I am truly so, so sorry."

Against his chest she said, "Oh my God, Shannon. They want to kill you. I can't take any more. I just can't take any more." He heard the despair in her voice. He felt her body drain of all its energy as she leaned against him.

He stroked her hair. "Shush, baby. It's gonna be all right. I promise it's gonna be all right. I got this. Don't worry."

Tawney pulled away from him. "No, Shannon. It's not going to be all right. I'm going to end up burying you next to Jazz." With those words went the last crack in Tawney's armor. A picture of the second coffin in her family to enter the ground flashed through her mind.

She screamed hysterically, beating her fist on the ground. "It's not fair. I'm sick of this. It's just not fair."

Shannon looked up at the sky. They sat in the middle of the street. He pondered Tawney's words. She was right, it wasn't fair. Life didn't seem fair sometimes. But only the strong survived. He could not allow her to go weak on him, because if she did there was every chance that they might not make it.

"Listen to me, Tawney. We're going to beat this . . ." Shannon's voice trailed off as he heard what he thought was the equivalent of a low rumble.

A Jeep was cruising slowly down the street. It picked up speed. Faster. Faster. Until . . .

Shannon squinted over the top of Tawney's head. "Dear Jesus."

The Jeep was coming straight at them. He snatched Tawney to her feet in one swoop. He gripped her wrist. "Baby, we're going to have to run for it."

"What?" Tawney said in confusion.

Suddenly she became aware of the roar of the Jeep. She looked back just as the Jeep rolled practically on top of them. Shannon jerked on her wrist, making her feet fly into motion.

The Jeep bore down on them. Shannon pulled Tawney with him onto the sidewalk. The Jeep jumped the curb, pursuing them without missing a beat. Sweat poured from Shannon's face, and his limbs ached from the earlier beating he had taken. He looked around swiftly, seeking shelter from the Jeep.

Ballistic's man Warren P. was at the wheel with Trey on the passenger side. Rasheem and Mitchell were two underlings who were trying to make their way up into the ranks. They sat in the backseat ready for the takedown.

Rasheem leaned out the window and pointed his trigger finger at Shannon. "Bang, Bang!" he shouted as the Jeep flew over a bump, leveling off. Rasheem leaned back in the Jeep laughing as a picture of Shannon's brains flying out of the other side of his head entered his mind.

Mitchell glared at him. He couldn't stand silly-ass niggas. He handed him a gun. "If you wanna take the nigga down quit pretending."

Rasheem shook his head. "No can do, man. Ballistic don't want us to touch him. Heads will roll. Trey gave the word. Right, Trey?"

Trey only nodded.

Trey was becoming increasingly uncomfortable with gangster life, yet he was a leader and always in the midst of it. It was like being on a roller-coaster ride that you couldn't climb off.

Warren P. pulled the Jeep so close to Shannon and Tawney that he could reach out and touch them if he wanted to. Instead he said, "Open the door, Mitchell. When I pull up next to them swoop up the girl."

He swerved the Jeep on the side of them. "Now!"

The door swung open and Mitchell grabbed Tawney from Shannon's grasp, pulling her into the Jeep. Tawney let out a shrill scream as she found herself separated from Shannon. The door slammed shut.

Tawney squirmed. Fear shot straight through her body at the dawning realization that she was at the mercy of these monsters without Shannon's help. She kicked at the window with all of her might.

Unbeknownst to her the window had been strengthened with reinforced glass, so she would definitely not be able to kick it out. This was unfortunate.

Shannon banged on the door of the Jeep, as a sickening feeling hit the pit of his gut. He tried to get Tawney back. He struggled for a grip on the window, but Warren P. accelerated, causing his tentative hold to be broken.

Mitchell struggled with Tawney, who was fighting him like an alley cat. He finally managed to put a rag over her nose and mouth, knocking the fight out of her. She went limp in his arms.

Shannon stumbled like a scarecrow in the wind on the side of the Jeep his legs dangling as he was completely cut off. He fell to the street as the Jeep raced off spraying glass and street debris all over him.

He heard hoots of laughter coming from the Jeep as it sped away from him with his wife as hostage. A feeling of doom permeated Shannon's entire being. It was like nothing he'd ever felt before, a tangible power unseen but felt. Waves of black washed over him.

Mama stepped out from behind the huge potted plant on her porch, where she'd been since she heard the screeching. She'd seen the whole thing. Shannon Davenport was going to need her help. She was an old woman but he needed her whether he knew it or not, very desperately.

His house had been shot up and destroyed, so he couldn't stay there. This was her shot and Mama had never been known to miss a shot. She wouldn't now either. She'd nurse Shannon

Davenport back to physical health. Then she'd school him in the spirit. Because without a doubt Mama suddenly knew this boy whom she'd practically watched grow up in the streets was the tool that would be used to set things right.

He was one of the ones who had sat at her table as well when he was young. He'd terrorized the streets, then done an about-face when he got himself a wife and baby. She'd admired him because he'd stayed in the neighborhood, bought a house to put his wife in and raise his child in. All in the neighborhood he'd grown up in.

Now this.

It suddenly occurred to Mama like a breeze on the wind that Shannon was different, always had been. And Mama always listened to the wind of her inner voice. One never knew which way it would blow. Yes, the Destroyer was in their midst. Had always been so. But so was the power. Had always been so, a two-sided coin it was.

Mama looked up in time to see the North Star twinkle. "I hear you, Lord," the old woman muttered under her breath.

Across the street Marcus Simms, who had been Jasmine's best friend, the same little boy who had watched her die on the street, as her blood ran from her body into the sewer, watched as the Jeep sped away. He watched Shannon, who was lying in the street, struggle to get to his feet.

Marcus went over, giving him a shoulder to lean on. He helped him to his feet. They didn't speak. There were no words.

Neither of them wanted to consider the fate of Tawney, who was most definitely in the clutches of evil.

Chapter 30

Warren P. pulled into a deserted industrial garage. The door closed behind them. Mitchell grabbed Tawney from the Jeep and threw her on the floor. The rest of them climbed out as well.

"Listen up, I need to meet with Ballistic. I need you two to stay on top of this situation until I come back," Trey said. He glanced at Tawney before putting an arm around Warren P.

"You can ride with me, G. Rasheem and Mitchell have got this." He pulled the hood of his sweatshirt over his head, tying a knot in it.

"Hold up. Is Ballistic going to want to be up on this?" Rasheem questioned. "She's personal, you know."

Trey nodded. "Yeah, I know. But nothing goes down in this city that Ballistic don't know about. You feeling me? Especially if his crew is involved."

Rasheem and Mitchell both nodded.

"Good." Remembering to be hard Trey said, "Wake that whore up, man. I don't want her out too long."

Warren P. chimed in. "Yeah, man, otherwise she'll turn into a vegetable from that poison you dosed her with." He laughed.

"We're raising up outta here, little man. Keep it tight until I talk to Ballistic."

"And you know that," Rasheem replied.

Trey and Warren P. exited the garage by a back door, leaving the Jeep as well. They were pretty sure that the Jeep was hot on the streets by now. They would have to get rid of it.

As soon as they heard the door close Mitchell said, "I guess we'd better wake up the Black Sleeping Beauty." He took a vial from the inside of his jacket. He stuck it under Tawney's nose, waving it around. She sputtered awake.

Rasheem leaned over, whacking her a couple of times across the face for good measure. "Wake up, Sleeping Beauty."

Tawney's eyes opened slowly. She tried to focus. When she finally did the leering face of Mitchell came into view. She shook her head slightly, hoping to stay the nightmare. It had only just begun.

Blurry-eyed Tawney saw a glistening shiny object on the inside pocket of Rasheem's leather jacket. She knew from the evil glint it couldn't be good. Her eyes opened wide in fear as she identified the knife.

Rasheem met her glance. His eyes traveled slowly and coldly from her head to her toes. He could taste her fear on his lips, and he was enjoying it.

He removed the knife from his pocket, sticking the blade to Tawney's face, drawing an imaginary line with it from the tip of her ear to her mouth. His eyes glazed over. "You ain't half bad-looking, you know that?"

Tawney turned her face away. Rasheem yanked it back. "I was told you're one of them upscale uppity niggas, the kind that read the *Wall Street Journal*. They also told me you were smart. Now would be a good time for you to put that to use. Don't ever turn away from me when I speak, ho."

He slapped her so hard her head reeled back. Tawney tasted blood in her mouth. But she was glad that nothing felt loose.

"You hear me?" he said while yanking on a fistful of her hair. Tawney didn't answer.

Rasheem spat in her face. "When I speak you answer." He slapped her again, then put his mouth to her ear so she could clearly hear him. "Did I hear you speak?"

Tawney managed a tightly controlled, hate-filled "Yes."
"That's better, dog."

Mitchell stepped in front of Tawney, pushing Rasheem to the side. He had a sadistic streak a mile long when it came to women. He had little to no respect for them, mostly because he'd watched his mama trick during most of his childhood. He hadn't been in school for two years since he was twelve. When he was there he was a complete terror. The teachers had long ago begun to pass him on just to get rid of him.

He didn't care. One day he did them all a favor and just stopped going. All he wanted to do was be tough and hard anyway. Besides, when Ballistic's reign was over he wanted to control Newark.

His aspiration was pure cash. He still listened to old-school Wu-Tang. That noise blared out of his Jeep when he was rolling down Clinton Avenue in search of his crew.

His favorite song was "C.R.E.A.M." (Cash Rules Everything Around Me). The song was a classic because no matter how much time went by he knew it was all the same just like the song said. He broke out rapping the lyrics of the song while Tawney stared at him. "Cash rules everything around me, everything around me, dollar, dollar bill, y'all."

He stooped down in front of Tawney. "So how much cash are you worth, Ms. Lady? How much can I get for you?"

Tawney shrank back from him. Sensually he stuck his finger in her mouth, swirling it around. Big mistake. Tawney bit down on his finger until she heard bones crack. Mitchell hollered, snatching his finger from her mouth. Red-hot heat swiftly ran through his body as his anger surged.

He punched Tawney like she was a man on the street. With that Tawney scrambled to her feet, swinging back. She threw him a couple of good blows. She was fueled by pure hatred and the disgust that this boy—because to her he was just a young punk boy—had no respect for her and she was a grown woman.

There was no way she was going to just let him have his way, so she decided to go out fighting. She swung on him, catching him square upside the head. Rasheem, who had been watching this exchange, was astonished at this wildcat broad. He couldn't believe his eyes. She was crazy. They didn't have time for this crap.

He dove for her legs, tackling her to the ground while Mitchell landed blow after blow to her body. But Tawney was strong and although she was at a disadvantage she was still kicking, screaming, biting, and throwing punches.

Finally tiring of her, Mitchell started to choke her. He had knocked out many a broad in his life just for getting smart with him, and this one thought she could go toe to toe with him. She was insane. This ho had lost it.

His hands were around her throat and he squeezed tighter and tighter. He was in a silent rage as he squeezed tighter. Tawney grew weaker and weaker from the lack of oxygen.

It was finally Rasheem who came to his senses as a picture of Ballistic flashed through his mind. They had a direct order not to mess with Shannon Davenport. Rasheem had a feeling that although that order hadn't extended to Shannon's wife, by virtue of her being his wife, if they killed her it might somehow interfere with Ballistic's plans and order.

If they did that they were dead meat. Better to err on the side of wisdom. Rasheem grabbed Mitchell from behind. "Yo, man, stop! You're going to kill her! We can't kill her!"

There was also the issue of the personal vendetta, which was a totally different spin that could get them body-dropped and killed as well if they blew this.

"I'm telling you, Mitchell."

Mitchell was so intently involved with watching Tawney lose air while her face changed colors that it was as though he were on a different planet and couldn't even hear Rasheem.

Rasheem gave a mighty yank from behind, pulling Mitchell completely off her, loosening his death grip around Tawney's neck in the process.

Tawney could barely gasp for air. Her entire stomach heaved from the violence, and its contents flew out of her mouth all over the floor.

She was still alive but she'd rather not have been. After all, this was only her first go-round with the devil. The highlight was yet to come.

Proverbs 1: 18 and 19: And they lay wait for their own blood; they lurk privily for their own lives. So are the ways of every one that is greedy of gain; which taketh away the life of the owners thereof.

Chapter 31

Trey and Warren P. watched as Ballistic paced back and forth. The chips were falling in place to his liking.

Trey spoke on Ballistic's cue that he was able to do so. "Rasheem and Mitchell have Davenport's wife. It's a personal favor in honor of Spence's death."

Ballistic nodded. "It is an ambitious move."

He was already aware of the circumstances and had been waiting to see how long it would take before the 411 was relayed to him. He knew they were pretty much on schedule as it should be.

"She's in a safe spot. We grabbed her off the street earlier. She should keep for a while."

Ballistic stroked his face. "I am rather pleased at the turn of events. It could work to our favor."

"How so?" Warren P. chimed in. Trey shot him a warning glance. Ballistic didn't miss it.

They were to speak only when spoken to. It was Ballistic's unwritten rule. Ballistic was thinking to himself that Trey had better school Warren. If he violated one more time he would swim with the fishes as the Italians used to like to say.

"You've done well." Ballistic went on as though Warren P. had never spoken. "There is one more piece left."

They both stood at attention. This time Warren P. had the

good sense to keep his mouth shut. He had detected imminent danger on his last question, and Trey's warning glance had reminded him of Ballistic's "speak only when you're spoken to," rule. He knew it wouldn't pay to be so zealous again.

"Take the woman to the old storefront on Clinton Avenue. Send Rasheem to Rico with the message about the woman and her whereabouts. Have him charge Rico for the information."

Trey smiled at the simple brilliance of Ballistic's plan. With a lift of his head, Ballistic indicated Trey could speak. He could feel him brimming to put the pieces together.

He rather liked Trey and considered him the wisest of the crew. He was seriously considering giving him a coveted position one day. His throat gurgled as he waited for Trey's response.

"Yeah, Rico knows Davenport will look for his wife and he won't make Rasheem's connection to us."

"Exactly."

Ballistic limped over to the chair with his cane to sit down. Immediately his German shepherd was at his side.

"Make sure that Shannon Davenport without a lot of effort knows where to find his wife. We'll be waiting for Rico when he shows up. Leave a trail on the kidnapping of Shannon's wife that leads straight to Rico. That'll clear the guilty party."

Ballistic waved his cane in the air. "I'm going to call in my markers with Rico's crew. What's left of them, that is. People owe me. It's time. Rico DeLeon Hudson will soon learn that I have purchased all that is his. It's time to take baby boy out for the count. I don't wish to waste any more time toying with him."

Ballistic agitatedly waved his cane in the air once again. "Leave me!"

There were times when he had enough of people. He was very much a loner. And this was one of those times.

Besides, he was being called on for a higher duty by that to which he paid his allegiance. He needed time to prepare for that ritual. He needed a council with the Darkling.

Chapter 32

Tawney was huddled on the floor in a tight ball in a corner of the garage when Trey and Warren P. returned. Trey glanced at her, assessing the damage. She was still breathing, so these two young bucks were still within their parameters. Although by the look of things they were skirting it pretty close.

They had made a mess of the pretty lady.

Trey brought them up to date. "I had a talk with Ballistic. He wants you to go see Rico Hudson."

"Why?" Rasheem asked, puzzled.

Their piece hadn't been connected to Rico at all even though word was all over the street that he and Shannon Davenport were beefing.

"He wants you to sell Rico information."

Rasheem raised an eyebrow. He glanced sideways at Mitchell. Mitchell lit a cigarette, listening intently. There might be a promotion or something in it for them. He couldn't wait to start getting some real cream. 'Cause cash ruled everything around him, and that was word.

"What kind of information?" Rasheem said.

"The final destination of Tawney Davenport. The old Clinton Avenue storefront."

"Yeah, we can do that. Rico will buy a little freelancing on our part. He knows we're about the cream." Rasheem grinned in Mitchell's direction, ecstatic at the opportunity to impress the all-important Ballistic.

Trey purposely hadn't told them about Ballistic's thinking the kidnapping played right into his plans, because he didn't want them getting bigheaded.

"Tell him you found a way to smoke Shannon Davenport out for him but it is going to cost him. It ain't no freebie. He'll jump at it because he's bugging about his girl's death and he can't get his hands on Ballistic. He's doing petty stuff for revenge."

"That's word," Warren P. said.

"We're getting the word on his actions, but he ain't even in the ballpark, so we know he's frustrated," Trey said, calling out Rico's situation.

"He's gonna be looking to waste some blood just to quench his thirst."

"Also you need to float the word over the wire, with the trail leading to Rico for the kidnapping of Tawney Davenport. We're going to reinforce Shannon's thought that Rico grabbed her. Also the wind doesn't need to blow in the direction from which it's really coming. You feeling me?"

"We're feeling you." Rasheem spoke for both of them.

"Got it?"

"Got it!" Mitchell and Rasheem replied in unison.

Trey handed them a huge knot of fresh one-hundred-dollar bills, then left the garage again on foot.

When Trey was gone Rasheem snatched Tawney to her feet. "It's time to roll on to your final destination, Ms. Thang."

Looking at him, Tawney saw nothing but death in his eyes.

Chapter 33

In one of the safe houses Rico, Temaine, and a few of the crew members were sitting around. There was a lot of nervous energy in the room. Sean, a short skinny dude who talked too much, stood watching Temaine.

He couldn't stand the sight of Temaine, never could. To him Temaine was arrogant and sly. He reminded him of a damned weasel. Slippery when it's wet. Sean never did trust him. Also he was sick of Temaine and that damned piece of licorice.

He always had that mess stuck in his mouth no matter what the situation was. He looked like an overgrown kid from day care. It was grating on Sean's nerves just looking at him. "Why you always sucking on that licorice, man?"

Temaine jumped up from his seat. He didn't say a word. He shoved Sean clean off his feet. Sean fell backward over some chairs, looking up at Temaine in surprise.

Temaine pulled his gun from his waistband, putting it to Sean's temple. "Shut up, nigga! I don't want to hear your stupid mouth no more."

It was kind of comical in a way because the piece of licorice was hanging from Temaine's mouth, yet the gun coupled with the frown on his face meant serious trouble.

Angrily Temaine clicked off the safety and twirled the barrel.

The other crew members rushed over yelling for Temaine to knock it off and take the gun away from Sean's head.

Rico's voice reigned supreme in the room, although he wasn't the least bit excited. In fact Rico was like the ultimate calm before a storm. He didn't even raise his voice. It was just the deadly serious tone of authority that laced it, which caught a person's attention. "Take the gun away from his head, Temaine."

Temaine's finger itched on the trigger. Rico stepped closer. He snapped his fingers. "Now, Temaine."

Temaine looked down into the sweat-drenched face of Sean. Slowly he removed the gun from his temple. He put the gun back into his waistband, climbing off him.

"I got a plan. Don't get antsy on me now," Rico said to him.

Temaine's breathing slowed down a bit. He took a blue scarf from his jacket pocket. He tied it around his head. "I want Shannon Davenport dead now. The police are all over him. Not tomorrow. Not the day after. I want him now."

Temaine turned to him. "And Ballistic too," he bluffed. "Their time is running out. There is no more time. The time is now."

Rico let him run his course. "I'll be calling the shots around here, li'l brother," he said.

"Then start calling them now, blood," Temaine retorted.

Rico made eye contact around the room. Guns clicked quickly into place, all trained on Temaine.

Temaine looked wildly around the room realizing too late that he had overstayed his welcome. "Oh? So it's like that, Rico? I been kicking it on the block with you nigga since we was knee-high. And you wanna take a nigga out like that, huh?"

Rico snapped his fingers. The guns disappeared. He took Temaine's head in both of his hands. He kissed him on the forehead and then took a step back. "In God we Trust."

A shot rang out from behind Temaine, hitting him in the back of the head. It dropped him to his knees. He looked up at Rico with shock in his eyes. He had played his last hand. "Why?" was the last word he uttered.

"Because you flipped sides, li'l brother," were the last words he heard.

Grief briefly flickered in Rico's eyes.

The words "rockabye, baby" instead of being screeched were being whispered in the winds of destruction. The bodies of the black-targeted babies were piling up. And the children of the damned unknowingly were preparing to fight back.

Marcus Simms got up from his spot outside the window where he had witnessed Temaine's demise.

Aisha, the poor child, was drenched in sweat. Great rolls of it cascaded down from her hairline into her face. Her vocal cords were still locked in silence. Yet though she couldn't speak on her sketchpad she continued to write in red marker. *Jesus! Jesus! Jesus!*

Unknowingly she was unlocking a floodgate in the spirit. She couldn't talk but she could write. *Jesus, Jesus, Jesus,* she scribbled in a frenzy.

Chapter 34

The Past

Satan is a liar. There is no truth in him. Although this has been mentioned throughout scriptural history time and time again, it is still the greatest form of deception known to man. As well as the most unaccepted one.

Neither the elders of the past nor the generations that would come forth into the present, or their offspring, which wound up being the children in Newark, were any different.

None of them believed any more than the rest of the world, and in keeping with that was the foundation of their disbelief in which most of their terror was laid as they lacked the power of bellief. The tracks of blood that were currently lining the streets of Newark, New Jersey, poured from their bodies.

The spirit demon rose up like a mist, shaking the trees just like it did when Jazz died in the gutter of their streets. Marcus Simms saw it. But still none of them would grasp the true source.

So when one woman's child was wrenched from her grasp, and sacrificed before her very eyes not moments before her own gruesome death, and when she vowed with her last breath of life to swap her soul in exchange for a haunting revenge, the people in attendance thought it was folly.

They thought it was a desperate woman's last cry for vengeance. Well, they were wrong. Satan, who is known by more names than can be listed here, but suffice it to say he is the same, was present as he always has been in the world's darkest hours.

He is of the principalities of darkness. He is the author of spiritual wickedness in high places. Ephesians chapter 6. It's all there. We wrestle not against flesh and blood, but against principalities, against powers of darkness, against the rulers of darkness of this world, against spiritual wickedness in high places.

But they just didn't believe.

So when Ms. Dorothy, as she was known, pierced the realms with her exchange request to become a spirit demon in exchange for her soul, her request was both heard and granted. It was that simple.

The rest, as you've been following—is history.

The night Ms. Dorothy and her baby were slaughtered is written in the spirit of black magic. There was a storm the likes of cats and dogs that night as water poured, not fell, from the skies. The night was as dark as a black ink spot, the kind of black where nothing moved, an inky, sticky black.

Streaks of lightning danced through the dark, like lit batons that had been strewn through the sky. The thunder rolled and cracked, like a sonic boom not from the heavens but from right there on earth, right next to your ear.

Everybody heard it. Including Mama, Papa, and Nana Mama, who were barely past the thumb-sucking, bed-wetting age at that time, and were the best of friends along with some of their other friends from the neighborhood who were now long since dead.

They should never have witnessed it, but being the hardheaded curious little kids they were, they had seen it all. They decided they wanted to see what was going on with Ms. Dorothy, because she was the talk of the Louisiana swamps and they were fascinated both by her and by the stories of her.

From their hiding place the three of them trembled together like little matchsticks as they witnessed the hideous display of a trial by judge and jury, and the occurring tragedy.

The woman's imminent demise was predicated on lies, on deception, on pure evil. None of the rumors, stories, or old wives' tales were true. It was the game of the beast exerting his power over man. Luring him into sinful territory, into damnation where he would have total control.

True to the game the lies were going to cost them their most prized possession, their souls. Though the body were dead the spirit had yet to live again, though not for the damned.

Ms. Dorothy was on her knees in the dirt-floor shack, in front of a flaming fire. Encircling her were a number of men and women all dressed from head to toe in black. Even their faces were covered; the only opening in the garment was the eyeholes.

This was so that in the small town no one would truly know who had really been responsible for what. Unless you recognized the soul of someone through the eyes. Because after all, the eyes are the windows of the soul.

It was their way of meting out justice, and covering the crimes of the guilty. Ms. Dorothy would forever remember the clothing they wore, as well as the eeriness of the black-clad figures, even after she left that body and became spirit.

At times in her darkest moments she would come to emulate it, black veil over the face and all. Only she didn't use eyeholes. With the strength of her sight in spirit form she could see through concrete, nevertheless through a veil.

This was what Shannon Davenport saw that day outside Je's Restaurant. Her black caricature so to speak. When she appeared in this form there was imminent danger as there had been on the night Shannon first witnessed her.

But what she would remember about that night more than anything was the wrenching away of her baby, the sacrificing of the bouncing brown-eyed baby boy who looked into her eyes, smiling and grabbing her finger to his mouth. A love supreme.

She would never forget his sweet baby smell, the instant gurgling, the joy, and the happiness that emanated from one small baby boy. Nor could she stop hearing the sound of his chuckle.

As all the forces, both those seen and not seen, looked on, one of the figures stepped forward, wrenching the baby from Ms. Dorothy as she clutched him tightly to her bosom cooing the lullaby "Rockabye, Baby" in his ear as she rocked him softly.

"Please," she begged. "You've made a mistake. It's not what you think. Take me but spare his life. I beg of you, spare his life."

Tears streamed down her cheeks as a look of pure terror flashed from behind eyes that were once woebegone, but now were filled with absolute disbelief and terror. The child had been the one real bright spot in her life.

The black-clad figure yanked the child from her grasp, causing the child to burst out screaming. She looked up with her tear-filled eyes. "For which crime do you charge me?"

"You have born a sacrifice birthed on that day in that hour. His blood is the blood of many," the black-clad figure replied.

"His blood is innocent," she retorted.

"His blood is spilled," responded the figure as he slashed the child's throat in one smooth motion, silencing the baby's cry at the same time. The baby's blood gurgled from the wound, dripping onto his mother's head and splattering across her clothing.

"His blood is a sacrifice. With his blood we pay so many others will not. The spilling of his blood will wash away the evil he has brought with his birth."

Ms. Dorothy hiccupped. "Rockabye, baby, rockabye, baby," she sang until she began to screech the words from the top of her lungs. "*Rockabye, baby, rockabye, baby.*"

She held out her arms for the dead child, but even in death he was not to fill them. Her outstretched arms were ignored.

Suddenly her chant of "Rockabye, baby" changed to a request. "Oh, Prince of Darkness, I commend you my soul," she prayed to the dark forces.

For an instant in time she was transported away from her enemies, where she bargained and sealed her own fate for revenge. She shook hands with the devil gladly. She traded all she had for the forces of darkness, and with her trade she would exact revenge.

Upon her being returned to her reality, the last words she spoke were "The blood of your offspring will be spilled in the streets. Damnation is written in their future."

She reached once again for the infant. "Rockabye, baby."

With those words she was pushed face-first into the flaming, searing fire. The sight of this woman burning alive was so horrid that the children who were watching vomited in unison, their stomachs heaving.

And they never forgot the words that rose up out of the fiery fire, out of the black-burned charcoal body that shouldn't have been able to speak but it did. *"I am the Darkling and I will remember you all!"*

"Rockabye, baby! Rockabye, baby!" Ms. Dorothy screeched even after death.

Chapter 35

The Darkling didn't accept misses, Ballistic learned when the spirit turned a deaf ear to him, because it missed collecting the soul of Kesha, Rico's lady.

Part of the Darkling's bargain with Satan was that he/she/it was to collect as many souls as it could for the kingdom of darkness. This was how Satan kept score with the Lord.

He loved to brag about the ones he'd stolen, lured, or enticed away from the Kingdom of Light. He'd known for a long time that the best he could do was trip them up, lead them astray, and place whatever stumbling blocks came to mind in their paths.

In the end it would come down to the scorecard. The only thing that amazed him is that they were too stupid to know it. This was a test. Scores of them had failed, leaving him victorious.

Fame, success, the scorning of poverty was all fodder for his grill. Like most black neighborhoods, Newark was easy to trade in. He loved it. It was so easy to instigate the young bucks, who were angry and brimming with rage at their place in society.

They believed this was all there was. Boy, were they going to be pissed off when they learned the truth—albeit it would be too late by the time it happened. He was a master at deception, and he was the creator of hunger; they just didn't know.

He'd invented game.

That's who he was, darkness and a lie. There was no truth in him and there never would be. That's why he traded with people like the Darkling, more soldiers in the foot army.

The Darkling's job in exchange for being a shape shifter with spiritual powers was to collect whenever there was a body drop. It missed because in the final moment of death Kesha stared the evil in the face, realizing they'd all been played. The tables had been turned.

Ballistic was stupid. He had no spiritual insight. He thought he could just drop bodies, but there had to be an aftermath for the Darkling to feed on, a soul to pass on as there had been with his stepfather, and many other bodies, but not with this one.

What Ballistic hadn't seen but what the Darkling had witnessed was the separation of the spirit from the flesh when his dog chewed the life out of Kesha.

Ballistic had missed the light that had shone, the powerful *hand* that reached out to the girl, all because in an instant she had uttered a prayer of forgiveness to the world's sacrificial lamb.

The lamb.

She had summoned the blood of the lamb.

Something the Darkling hadn't done when she was human, being consumed with black hatred, rage, and foaming at the mouth with a taste for the blood of her enemies. Once Kesha had evoked a plea for mercy the Darkling had howled in abject pain, as she'd lost the possession of the girl's soul to give to her maker.

In the flesh Kesha had fallen victim; in the spirit she had overcome and been rendered untouchable. She had called the name of Jesus. There was power in that name.

Really.

The Darkling trembled at the sound of the Prince of princes' name being called. And it was always the same when it happened—complete defeat.

Now Ballistic stood trying to evoke her powers, the Darkling's powers, her spirit in a deadpan ritual, so he could be cleansed and empowered to continue his reign of terror.

She had answered him long ago, feeling a kinship for his hunger for revenge, but on this night she was incensed over the miss.

The Darkling didn't accept misses, so on this night as she watched Ballistic she left him on his own, knowing that he would pay for not delivering. Yes, if you danced to the music, sooner or later you would pay the piper. Ask your mama.

Ballistic watched the last embers of the fire die, wondering why he felt incomplete on this night.

His cell phone rang. He picked up, receiving the news of Bobby's death. Rico had made quite a spectacle of the boy in exchange for the dead Kesha. He had dropped a piece of Bobby's body off at each of Ballistic's safe houses and Rico's stickup boys had taken whatever dope and cash were in the houses.

Ballistic smiled to himself. Newark had always had the most notorious reputation in the country for their stickup boys. Even New York wasn't on the map when it came to stickups.

Hell, Newark's stickup boys had been known to rob cats in New York, leaving a trail of fear, and they'd better not even think of coming to Newark for revenge.

Otherwise their new graves would be Port Newark or maybe they'd float back to the city via the Hudson River. It all depended on the crew and the mood.

Ballistic would have to alert Trey and Warren P., Bobby wasn't a main hit, and neither were any of the houses, but it was close enough for that punk Rico. Ballistic had it locked, copped, and blocked, but sometimes there were failures. It was all part of the game.

He hit up Trey and Warren P., telling them to watch their backs. His eyes and the eyes of the German shepherd turned red simultaneously. Letting out a howl like a wolf keening in the night, he summoned the Darkling once again.

And once again he received no answer.

Chapter 36

The next day at the bank Dominique was just about to leave the ladies' room stall when she heard Shonda's voice. Instinctively she stepped back against the stall listening.

Shonda gave her the creeps down-low seriously. She had told Tawney long ago to transfer her or do something to just get rid of her, but Tawney only laughed. Tawney didn't think Shonda's attitude was all that serious.

But Dominique knew a snake when she saw one even if it was dressed in banker's clothes.

Shonda and Debbie walked into the lounge, continuing their conversation. Shonda, whose instincts were usually on a par with the devil's, didn't sense Dominique. In fact she never bothered to even look to see if anyone else was in the lounge.

Debbie was busy trying to fight her way out of the cocoon of Shonda's madness. She went to the sink to wash her hands, thought better of it, and stopped to stare at Shonda as though she were crazy.

"Girl, are you out of your mind? That mouth of yours is going to get you in trouble one day," Debbie stated emphatically. She couldn't believe her ears. Shonda was talking pure insanity.

Shonda stared arrogantly at her reflection in the mirror. "I ain't lying. Gangsters have kidnapped Tawney. Rico's crew. I told you that husband of hers used to be a gangster. I tried to tell you that all that glittered wasn't gold, but you ain't believe me," Shonda said with what could not be mistaken for anything except malice.

Shonda shrugged nonchalantly. Debbie washed her hands. Shonda's eyes wandered from her own reflection in the mirror to Debbie's. "Word," she said.

"No. I don't believe you." Debbie reached for a paper towel, drying her hands. "You're talking trouble. Real trouble. So I suggest you shut up. I don't want to hear any more, Shonda. And I'm dead serious. Keep your filthy lies to yourself. Somebody's gonna get hurt listening to you."

Shonda laughed. She pulled out a nail file, buffing her nails. "You're a straight-up punk, Debbie. You ain't stand-up, girl. Where I come from you've got to represent."

Dominique barely breathed as she listened to the exchange. Debbie shook her head. "I thought you wanted a career. You're about to kill it with that mouth of yours."

"I ain't killing anything. Tawney was killing it for me anyway with that lethal pen of hers writing me up with bad performance reviews and messing with my money."

Shonda blew on her nails. "Besides, the bank may need someone to take her place now. No doubt when them niggas finish with her she won't be coming back."

A look bordering on insanity flashed in the depths of Shonda's eyes. The familiar light peeked out, and this time Debbie didn't miss it. She backed up a step, wondering how it was they'd never seen it before.

Shonda smiled serenely.

She could smell the fear that suddenly emanated from Debbie. It was like a liquid stench coming from her pores. Shonda was a predator. Predators always knew when they had a weaker animal cornered.

But Debbie wasn't in the eye of her storm so she let it go, using her for an information source instead. "Is Tawney at work today?"

Debbie suddenly frowned. "No."

"I rest my case." Shonda pivoted on her stiletto heels, leaving Debbie to trail behind her.

Dominique stood frozen in the ladies' room stall in disbelief and fear. Although she couldn't stand the acid-tongued Shonda, something in her words rang eerily true.

Dominique needed to get the word out to send some help for Tawney like yesterday. She flipped through her mental Rolodex, trying to decide who it would be best to tell.

Time was not on her side.

Chapter 37

Rasheem stood outside in the graffiti-covered, dark gloomy hallway of Rico's latest safe house. All the young men in the hall were strapped and armed. Rasheem stood in the midst of enough artillery to blow up a city block.

He eyeballed the dude guarding the door as the line of flunkies flanked him. "I need to see Rico. I know he's in there." Rasheem patted down his dreads. As he did so he heard *click, click,* and *click.*

He realized that in that instant his brains could've been scattered across the floor like scrambled eggs simply because he'd had a vain moment of patting his hair.

It was a habit that was hard to break. He returned his hands to his sides. Rico's crew didn't relax. They kept the guns trained on him.

Very leisurely the dude guarding the door spoke. "Knowing too much can get you killed."

Rasheem didn't flinch. "Not knowing things can get you killed too."

His point wasn't wasted on the young man; he saw respect and acknowledgment flicker in his eyes. He smiled and tapped a code on the door.

When the door was opened he whispered in the young buck's ear. The door slammed shut. In a few minutes the door opened again and the boy inside nodded his head for Rasheem to enter. Rasheem was patted down once again for safe measure, then allowed to enter.

Rico stood in the center of the room as Rasheem entered. "State your business."

"This is going to cost you cash, Rico."

Rico narrowed his eyes. "What am I buying?"

"The lease on Shannon Davenport's life."

"Are you selling the lease on Ballistic's life too?"

Rasheem couldn't help but break a grin. "You're a funny man, Rico. Naw, I ain't got that dog."

Rico nodded. "Didn't think so."

He knew a petty street gangster like Rasheem and his running partner, Mitchell, couldn't shine shoes on the same street Ballistic walked on, but he was feeling himself a bit since he'd started hitting that bastard.

And no matter how much paper he had to spread he'd run up on B., as he'd started to think of Ballistic, sooner or later . . .

It was all in a matter of time. He snapped his fingers. A brown envelope filled to the brim appeared in his hands. Rasheem's eyes glittered with greed. That's what he was talking about, raking in the cream. Mitchell was going to wet his pants when he saw this stash.

"May I reach into my pocket?" Rasheem said respectfully.

"It's your life," Rico retorted.

Rasheem retrieved a piece of paper with the address on it where Tawney Davenport was being held. He handed it to Rico. "Shannon Davenport's wife, Tawney, is being held at that address. I figure he'll come for his wife. Don't you?"

Rico smiled.

In one swift moment the money was in Rasheem's hands. Rasheem turned to go. There was no thought for the woman's life he'd just sold.

Rico DeLeon Hudson watched him go. Shannon Davenport. He would end this punk's life and move on, gathering his rep in the dust of the old-school punk's ashes.

Chapter 38

Shannon Davenport was recovering from his wounds. But the ache in his heart over Tawney's kidnapping would not be stilled. He looked over to find Marcus sitting on Papa's footstool watching him intently.

The little brother had proved to be quite manly in the face of adversity. He'd helped Shannon hobble over to Mama and Papa's house on Mama's instructions after Shannon was injured.

Marcus had consistently been keeping an eye on Shannon since they arrived as though he thought Shannon might disappear into thin air.

He was also biding his time. Like the elf he could be at times, Marcus had obtained what Shannon would most desire. Like a shadow he had flitted in and out of the bloodcurdling streets, until he had what he needed.

Marcus remembered Jazz's blood running in the sewer. He could see it just as clearly as the day it had happened, like a river running.

He saw the same image every day and every single night, Jazz's life slowly seeping out of her, trickle, trickle, and trickle, into the dirty sewer.

This one was for her. That's why he had obtained what her

daddy needed most. Marcus felt old beyond his years, and his thoughts were light-years ahead of his physical age.

Jazz.

He shivered. He could still hear the shrieking that ripped through the air on the day she'd died. He had felt something morbid, clammy in the air. He couldn't explain it, but it was there.

And not one person had come right away. Marcus felt a sharp pang in his heart, realizing once again as he had on that day that no one really cared about them.

Even now he could hear Jazz's blood crying from the streets, from down in the dirty gutter where it had seeped, though not for revenge but rather amazingly for peace.

This was going to be tricky, he thought. He wished he understood more about what was going on. But mostly it was just a feeling. Things were being turned upside down.

Everybody knew in the hood it was an eye for an eye. Usually. Marcus shook his ten-year-old head as though his own thoughts were too much for him to bear.

"Marcus, there's a chopped barbecue sandwich, some potato salad, along with a slice of butter pound cake and strawberry ice cream, waiting for you on the table." Mama's voice sliced through Marcus's reverie as though it were being dispatched through satellite.

Marcus smiled, jumped to his feet, and headed without a word to the kitchen. When Mama put food on the table, you just went, plain and simple.

Shannon eyed the old woman, admiring her finesse. She had spent every moment since his beat-down nursing him back to health, and he had known it hadn't been without reason. But now it was time for her to cut to the chase because he needed to get on about his business, and the first thing he had to do was find his wife, hopefully alive. A murderous rage beat against his rib cage at the thought.

"Your home is at risk as long as I'm in it."

"More souls would be at risk if you were not."

Shannon hauled his propped-up legs from the table, leaning forward. "Mama, I ain't a man that's good with wordplay. And I don't know a thing about anybody's soul, including my own. I will need to leave your home under the cover of darkness. That will happen tonight. If there's something you need to say, it'd best be now."

Mama grunted, then sighed. "Boy, as old as you is, don't you knows yet that the spirit can't be rushed? I swear to all that be, this generation ain't got no learning."

Shannon felt beads of sweat pop out on his back. He didn't know if it was from the physical pain of the brutal beating he had withstood, or from an internal fear that sprang up inside him when Mama had mentioned the word *spirit*.

"I don't have any time to waste."

"You don't have any to give either," Mama stated astutely.

Shannon sucked in his breath, closed his eyes, and leaned his head back on the cushion of the couch. "What do you want from me?"

"All that is required."

"The only thing required of an old-school gangster is his blood, Mama."

"Then I guess today is a new day. The spirit doesn't want your blood. That's already been shed."

Shannon decided to humor the old woman. "Then, what does it want?"

"Your allegiance."

Thunder crackled. A cement block the size of a tall wall crumbled. Both Mama and Shannon made the visual connection at the same time.

The child was placed before them. They could see her clearly. Aisha Jackson. She scribbled one name. *Jesus*. The entire wall came tumbling down.

A layer of Shannon peeled slowly away and in that instant he knew he was expected to fight a war with nothing more than a child and a pen.

Mama searched his eyes. "Care to know why?"

Chapter 39

Aisha sat with her knees pulled up to her chin, trembling. Cold beads of sweat formed a neat line across her brow. The child's vocal cords ached from her not being able to speak. At times they throbbed as though she wanted to say something but couldn't.

She rocked back and forth trying to comfort herself. The source of her discomfort was in the air, heard but not seen. It was the baby crying. The baby had been crying for a half hour, a pitiful wail, longing, searching. It was everywhere and yet nowhere.

Aisha could hear the baby clearly. Only there wasn't a baby, there were only his cries and only she could hear him. Her mother had come into the room and noticed not a thing out of the ordinary.

Aisha wanted to scream at her, "Mommy, can't you hear the baby crying?" But screaming was impossible except within the walls of her mind because she couldn't speak, couldn't even whisper, so she certainly couldn't scream.

So in place of the scream that never left her lips her vocal cords throbbed with the sensation, with the desire to speak, but nothing came forth, nothing but the rocking, the beads of sweat on her forehead, and the wild knocking of her heart against her tiny chest.

Since Jazz had been killed their world had gone crazy. Aisha thought of Marcus. He was suffering too. And he was always alone now. Whenever she saw him from her window he was withdrawn and despondent, not lively like when they used to play hide-and-seek.

In fact there were no street games being played these days. The entire street was on a death knell. Aisha stayed in her room watching from the window. The few kids who ventured outside since Jazz's death mostly just sat on the curb, or stared listlessly at each other.

The laughter was gone. In its place was darkness and fear. Every child on the block had the same thought. *Would they be next?* How much of their blood had to be spilt in order to pay penance? Revenge was its own judge. Who would stop it? The generational hex was upon them and it had brought with it the sins of the past.

Over in Mama and Papa's house Papa's bones shook as he sat in a corner of his and Mama's bedroom reliving the day the Darkling was born over and over again. He would never forget the woman's cries of anguish, the pleading in her voice, nor the fear that shook her as hatred shrouded the last minutes of her life.

And most of all were the two crippling visions that simultaneously visited his mind, heart, and soul—the bright warm blood dripping from the slashed throat of the baby and the sight of his mother's face being pushed into flames of fire. "Dear Lord!" The words rushed from Papa's spirit before he realized he'd spoken.

Back in Aisha's room the baby howled loudly!

Aisha clambored from her spot on the bed. She got down on her knees on the side of the bed looking underneath it as she was sure this time that that was where the howling had come from. There was nothing under the bed but dust.

Tears ran in rivulets down Aisha's cheeks. The tears ran in rivulets down the dead baby's cheeks too. Aisha just couldn't see him for now.

Chapter 40

*C**are to know why?*

He hadn't but Mama had told him anyway. Shannon stared at Mama wordlessly after hearing the spine-tingling account of the very dark past of a woman, spirit demon, male or female thing, whatever you'd want to call it, and how her haunting sacrifice coupled with a tremendous personal loss might be affecting all of their lives.

They were surrounded in treacherous waters.

It was without doubt the most incredible story he had ever heard. Was it possible that his daughter might be dead because of a legendary curse, passed through the generations like a coveted inheritance?

As much as he'd like to deny its truth he couldn't. A black chill had run clean through his bones as Mama steadfastly relayed her account of the tragic event. Papa and Nana Mama, Shonda's grandmother, were in attendance as well. The spooked look in their eyes testified to the accuracy of Mama's memory.

Finally Shannon found his voice. "They spilt innocent blood over a rumor?"

Papa looked deep into Shannon's eyes. "Ain't that what y'all is doing every day in the streets now, son?"

Shannon leveled a gaze at the old man.

"Yes, sir, it is. But it's hard to believe that because of the day and hour that a child was born, people believed it was evil and slaughtered it, believing the mother was a witch as well. She sounds like nothing more than a poor woman who bore a child out of wedlock.

Nana Mama, who hadn't uttered a word the entire time, spoke up. Her real thoughts on the situation burst forth after seventy-some-odd years. "I always believed they done shed the blood of a prophet."

The only sound that could be heard was an intake of breath. Shannon could suddenly hear the quiet. You could've dropped a pin and it would have landed in their midst like a bomb. For the first time he realized that the Central Ward itself was quiet.

There were no street noises. No bullying sirens coming forth. No banging beats from the last of the quarters or whatever they called themselves these days from the hip-hop crew.

He wasn't politically correct or anything, but it still amazed him how people whose ancestors had been sold and exchanged like so much merchandise could wear monikers and names that amounted to change from a dollar bill. Damn, he must be getting old.

In any event there wasn't noise of any kind from beyond, and that was strange. No screeching tires, no screaming kids, and no hip-hop beats, no guns being fired, no collage of angry, belligerent voices riding the airwaves. Yes, this was extremely unusual; in fact, it was almost unheard of.

The Central Ward rocked twenty-four-seven. There was no such thing as quiet except in this one rare moment when an old woman had uttered words that no one else in that entire span of time had dared to even think.

Papa uttered, "It wouldn't be the first time in history we crucified innocence."

"If'n they did, Ms. Dorothy traded in her white robe for darkness and she's sworn on revenge and death. The blood of the forefathers is all over the streets of Newark through the seeds of their generations just like she promised," Mama said.

Nana Mama sighed. "Ain't nothing going to stop her."

Mama rocked in her chair. "There's one thing that will."

Three sets of eyes stared at her. "What's that?" Shannon said.

Mama's eyes rolled in the back of her head. All you could see were the whites of her eyes before she spoke. "It will take the innocence and belief of one man's heart to stop the hate. A child is where it began, and a child is where it will end."

Chapter 41

The old storefront on Clinton Avenue was covered in black paper. Years and years before it had been an old furniture warehouse. Since then it had become one huge dungeon, with halls that echoed, spiderwebs that clung to the corners of the mildewed ceilings, and rats running around the place.

Most of it was boarded up. The few windows that weren't boarded up were covered in black paper.

The streets on this night were deserted almost as though a pathway had been cleared for the evil that would take place. A space had been cleaned and altered inside the warehouse for this very special occasion.

The entire space had been recreated to reflect a municipal courtroom. This is where the trial would take place.

Unlike most trials in this particular courtroom, there was only a one-person judge and jury. There was no defense and there was no prosecution available, to present each side. There was only one side to this sordid crime, and there was only one judge who would preside. This courtroom didn't have the archaic systematic props found in most courtrooms.

The trial would be real, the way it should be minus the delays, props, and grandstanding. The parade of liars usually found at these events would not be present. Well, there was one liar but she would pay because there was only one judge, and that judge was *the* judge, jury, and public opinion all rolled into one.

Tawney sat at what would have been considered the defense table. Only she had no one to defend her and she was just about to come into this dark realization. Her hands were tied tight behind her back. Her feet were bound together.

She faced the judge's bench.

A massive headache was pounding inside her head; a sharp pain was beating just at the right side of her temple. Slowly she squeezed her eyes shut trying to still the pain, and absorb her surroundings. She was half asleep and groggy.

Shonda stood before Tawney in absolute supreme mightiness dressed in a black judge's robe. She took the pitcher of cold, dirty water sitting prepped and ready on the defense table, and threw it in Tawney's face.

Tawney sputtered awake, her eyes opening wide. She tried to move, but it was an effort as her circulation was being cut short by the binding on her hands and feet.

In slow motion as though a reel of film were being shown frame by frame, Tawney took in her surroundings. Finally her eyes came to rest on Shonda.

She had a hard time hiding her shock.

"That's better," Shonda said, glad to have Tawney's eyes on her, and reveling in her full attention. She watched Tawney's expression change from disorientation to confusion to a cagey trapped look of fear and uncertainty.

Shonda's heart sang. This was exactly where she wanted Ms. Thang. She made her way slowly, arrogantly, and with total command of the situation back to the judge's bench.

She was proud of her boys. The crew had done her proud recreating this room. She'd be damned if it didn't look just like Newark's criminal courtroom downtown. She knew because she'd checked.

This stage had to be perfect. What good was a show that wasn't real or authentic? Tawney was about to get a taste of Caesar's law Shonda style.

It was too bad there hadn't been time to carve some of those stone images that graced some of the older city buildings into these walls so every effect would be in place for Tawney's sentencing.

But alas, time would not allow for this.

Shonda sat down behind the bench. With an amused smile she watched Tawney struggle against the ropes. It was no use as Tawney soon learned. Shonda smiled again. She tilted her head, relishing the hate that flowed threw her veins at the sight of Tawney's predicament.

Finally she banged the gavel. "Court is in order."

Tawney stared at her in shocked disbelief. She blinked as though the image in front of her would disappear. It didn't. She shook her head, closing her eyes. Opening them she found the disastrous scene was still there.

She didn't know what was worse, Rasheem and Mitchell or being trapped with Shonda. But she did know that she had never had a nightmare that was as bad as this.

Looking around she took in the full effect of the newly erected courtroom. Her heart skipped a beat in fear. She could not fathom what was going on with Shonda, but something was deeply, disturbingly wrong.

"My God, Shonda. Are you crazy?"

Shonda left the judge's bench in a rage. She was so angry that her hair stood on end as though it were brittle. Spit formed in the corner of her mouth.

As she approached, Tawney felt a wave of hatred and vile contempt that was like a physical whip reaching out and snapping its sharp end at her. Waves of that contemptuous anger rolled off Shonda, as though they were waves frolicking in an ocean or crashing against the rocks.

Standing before Tawney she picked up the pitcher that had held the cold dirty water and hit Tawney in the head and face with it. Fortunately it was plastic, but it still made its mark as Tawney endured the brunt of Shonda's hate, unable to defend herself, or shield her head or face in any way.

Just to add insult to injury Shonda, tiring of the pitcher, threw it down, backhanding Tawney. She listened to Tawney's head snap. Then she strode back to the judge's bench.

"You're crazy," Tawney muttered in pain.

"Shut up. This is my courtroom and I'm the judge and the jury. Your high and mighty ass had better not forget that, whore."

Tawney saw pure insanity gleam from Shonda's eyes. Something dark and sinister peeked out from their depths, like a glimpse of darkness coming to the light. Looking closer Tawney saw the emptiness that Shonda's eyes reflected back.

All she could recall was Dominique's warning that something was wrong with Shonda, but it was too late now.

Quickly Tawney's thoughts flitted all over the place trying to find a solution to dealing with this psychopath, but she failed to find one. Shonda had expertly concealed her contempt and true personality.

She was in fact insane.

And her unbalance and insanity had gone unnoticed for too long. It had been covered beneath a corporate shield, and now that that shield was not in place; it shone brilliantly from its own pit.

In this dim aftermath Tawney slowly realized she would not be able to reason with insanity. Insanity was an illness that took no thought for others, and registered no emotion.

It fed on its need to shine, to glimmer, to control, and most of all to retain its very stature, and that was insanity. Within its world there was only one side, the side that it saw, and that was it.

It didn't matter, she couldn't give up. If she did she would surely die. "Why are you doing this, Shonda?" Tawney honestly couldn't imagine, but the question bore asking. Nothing she had ever seen in Shonda had prepared her for coming up close, face-to-face in a situation such as this one with her.

Shonda sat back in her seat, comfortable in her new role as judge. She liked this God-like feeling of sitting on top of the world, with all the minions below at her beck and call. She didn't know why she hadn't thought of this sooner. This was where she belonged, on top.

She reached beneath the bench and pulled out a stun gun, placing it next to her beloved gavel. Looking lovingly at the gavel, she picked it up and banged it once again for effect. Tawney jumped. She'd better jump if she knew what was good for her.

Shonda fingered the stun gun, relishing visions of Tawney's reaction once she stuck it to her skin. That scrawny muffin would buckle from the shock, and her hair would stand on end.

Watching her face and registering Shonda's emotions and thoughts, Tawney closed her eyes wishing hard that this situation would disappear. She knew that it wouldn't.

"Did you ask why?" Shonda finally addressed Tawney's question. She laughed a dry humorless laugh. "Because you are being charged, girlfriend."

"With what?"

Savoring the moment Shonda picked up her Uzi, which had been lying on the other side of the bench. She fired off a shot over Tawney's head, because the heifer had asked her that stupid question.

She couldn't believe Tawney was playing dumb with her, but so be it; before it was all over with she'd wish that she hadn't. Shonda was nobody to play with, and Tawney was about to learn that the hard way.

"Count one—betrayal to your hood." Another shot whizzed past the left side of Tawney's face.

"Count two—betrayal to your race." The next shot landed underneath the defense table between Tawney's legs. She almost wet herself.

"Count three—being a sellout nigga. I gotta tell you this is the worst offense of all, ho." This time she had damn near shot Tawney right in her stupid face. She had to stop herself almost on a dime, swerving the gun for another shot past the right side of her face instead.

She didn't want to end this too quickly. That would take all the fun out of things. She noticed that Tawney did not wear fear kindly. Gone were that arrogant attitude, beauty, and grace with which she carried herself.

In its place was a scared, fragile, ugly, and twisted rag doll.

Which is all Tawney had ever been with some cover girl makeup and *Fashion Fair* flair, in her opinion.

Yeah, that's what she was, a skinny, ugly rag doll. Look at her now, all twisted up in fear. She was a punk-ass heifer if Shonda had ever seen one.

Suddenly Shonda rose.

She roamed around behind the bench. Tawney watched her every move warily. "You're supposed to stand when I come into the room, you know."

"But you're a spoiled brat buppie. What would you know about that?"

Shonda continued pacing as though Tawney weren't even in the room. She lost focus on Tawney for a moment.

It was too bad Tawney couldn't have used the time to free herself, but it was pretty much useless. Shonda knew her stuff and Tawney couldn't escape.

Shonda began to twirl as Tawney watched in shocked amazement. "I am very pretty, you know."

Twirl. "I was a 4.0 average in college. Did you know that?" No response was required on Tawney's part, and Shonda wouldn't have heard her anyway. For the time being she had drifted into a place that only she inhabited.

Twirl. "With a 4.0 I could have been a Supreme Court judge one day." Suddenly she frowned. "I think . . ." Sighing she let it go for now.

Twirl. "I always got good write-ups on my performance reviews too. I was always the best at all that I did. My mama always told me there wasn't anything I couldn't do."

The twirling stopped.

"She was a lying witch of a mama if I ever seen one, though. She only told me that so I'd bed down with those niggas she wanted to strip for some cash. That witch was all about the paper."

Shonda's eyes roamed around the room unfocused. "That's why she's dead now. That's what happens when you use people, you get dead, you know. How many people do you know that have killed their mamas, Tawney?" She threw her head back laughing.

She was back in focus now.

Tawney was not only astonished at the level of Shonda's insanity, but also even in her current state of utter fear Shonda's sudden change in grammar shocked her.

"You're gonna get dead too, very soon, Tawney. I'm gonna give you some time to think about how I'm going to kill you. And then I'm gonna give you the verdict for your crime."

"From there we'll move on to your sentencing. In the meantime look there." Shonda pointed.

In a far-off corner Tawney couldn't believe what she was seeing with her own eyes. Hanging from a lightbulb in the ceiling was a noose.

Lest you should forget, you are in the alternate world of Out A' Order. It is a world of its own making. Even though there is a bulb shining brightly in this room do not be fooled because there is nothing but darkness.

Close your eyes. I will take you there.

Chapter 42

*Y*ou are traveling at the speed of light. So fast your eardrums are blocked and popping. The oxygen in the air is very little. The air is thin. You are going to a place that you have been running from all your life and that you did not want to believe existed.

In this place it is as black as midnight. And that in itself is the problem because in this place there should be only light. The light has been given and promised. Rejected. It has also been born, it has died, and then it has been born again.

There is a thief who broke in and stole the light. It is up to you to regain it. That is why you are now in darkness. That is also why I have brought you here. Follow the thread. You must listen to the right voice.

The realm in which you are now walking is the human mind. Only it isn't an average human mind, nor is it of ordinary thinking. It is built on depravity, a skewed sense of seeing things, and a balance for reasoning known only unto itself. It is certainly not within the known boundaries that we live in.

Keep walking because the tunnels you see here are sealed off. They are sealed in blackness, which means not even the faintest of light filters through.

Imagine a hallway that you desperately need to get out of. You've got to get out because if you don't you will die. You are being pursued. You can't see it, feel it in the physical, or touch it. Yet you know it's there, right behind you, breathing down your neck. You can now feel the heat and the stench of it in your face.

You see the exit sign leading out, but just as you near it you discover it disappears.

It was a mirage. In reality you are sealed off.

There is no exit, only a veil of black, like heavy drapery hanging suspended before you. There isn't a ripple of an opening in the drapery. It just goes on and on, for endless miles. Frantically you search for an opening. Your fingers hope to find the tiniest of threads to break through. You find none.

Look over there to the left. Normally there would be a sign that says Stop. Within these walls the sign is missing. It is missing because it isn't there. There is absolutely no stop sign. It doesn't exist.

Try looking to the right. There could have been a sign saying Merge, but there isn't. With whom would you merge? There are no others here like you. There is only the blackness. You can't even see your own hand in front of you, although it is by this hand that you might die.

If you walk straight ahead you might run into Pain, and he would've told you that that would hurt, except he isn't there to say so, and besides, it would've been too late. You've already run into the hand that might kill you.

If you do a complete turnaround maybe you'll bump into Morality, except that won't happen because she isn't home. Don't even bother to reach overhead to see if Respect is in the house, because I know you know at this point that he isn't.

Respect doesn't live here anymore.

You are an invited guest into the walls of Shonda Hunt's mind. Within these walls lives only darkness. There are other things that live here as well. I said this was Shonda's mind, but it could in fact be the mind of many. Perhaps it is. Or maybe it isn't so.

How can you tell the difference between the truth and a lie?

The thumping that you hear but cannot see is the thirst for revenge. My God, it's so loud that it is pounding like the beat of a drum. It is lust, it is murderous, it is competitive, and it knows no bounds. It's parked in the home spot and has been a feeding ground for itself for many a year. Remember what I said about following the right voice.

And the beat goes on.

Now that I've brought you here, I have a responsibility to bring you out. But I know you'll visit again in your own mind. That is how it goes with things that are unforgettable.

This is the world of Out A' Order. It rules. Don't be deceived by those who are caught up in it. They look like you and me. Such is the deceitful brilliance of darkness.

However, if you listen intently you will hear the right voice. It lies in the sound of thunder.

Chapter 43

The stun gun shocked Tawney into a state of awareness. An electrical bolt shot through her body that caused the area behind her eyes to burn.

Her body shook from the effect.

Before she could recuperate Shonda tagged her again, this time only lightly on the arm as she engaged herself in the enjoyment of Tawney's torture, as well as her helplessness. She didn't want to hit her with a lightning bolt that would turn her into a corpse just yet.

Pulling Tawney's head back to look into her eyes she said, "I've decided to skip right to the final verdict of guilty."

She paused.

"For your crimes you will be slowly hanged so I can watch your fear in nanoseconds."

Tawney tried to shake Shonda's grasp and get to her feet. She made a minute amount of progress before she fell back to her seat. Shonda slapped her face for her efforts. Tawney's eyes shot hot sparks of hatred at her.

Shonda threw the stun gun on the table. She backed up, throwing her hands in the air with major attitude. The robe swung around her as though parodying the death executioner that she was.

"I had Spence be rather merciful with Jasmine. I can guarantee you the same won't happen for you."

A distant ringing started in Tawney's ears as though it were echoing from far away. Even through her pain she knew she must have heard Shonda wrong. Everything was beginning to get all mixed up in her mind because of the madness of these events.

"What?" she said to Shonda in a disbelieving tone.

Shonda searched her face. There was no indication that Tawney had even remotely connected to or believed what she'd just said. In fact it could have been almost as though she hadn't spoken. Perhaps she'd better make it loud and clear for this heifer.

A weird shrill sound escaped Shonda's mouth sounding very much like a shriek from the Darkling before she spoke again. "What are you, deaf? I said that your ass won't receive the kid glove treatment given to the dead little princess.

"You should have seen the view from Spence's scope up on the roof. Jasmine could have been in the lens of a camera, but she wasn't. Although it was a Kodak moment."

"She looked just like a little princess with red ribbons all in her hair, before she got blasted and ended up with a hole in her chest, and her arms spread-eagled like she was a bird that could fly, but she wasn't. And I can testify to the fact that she couldn't fly and she damn sure didn't grow wings."

Tawney stopped breathing.

She looked at Shonda in petrified horror. This time she heard her, really, really heard her. Her body trembled. She felt a fluid surging through her body like ice water being poured into her veins. She struggled to free herself to no avail.

Having center stage, Shonda pranced around the room narrating a vengeful stream of viciousness for Tawney that most mothers could never have even dreamed of in their worst nightmare.

"Yeah, Ms. Holier Than Thou. You're the reason your daughter got hit. Your precious little Jazz, the one you can't stop talking about at work. It makes me want to throw up."

Shonda mimicked her. "Jazz did this and Jazz did that. Well, Jazz isn't going to do a damn thing anymore, Tawney. Is she?" she shrieked.

"Hell naw, she isn't because she's gone now. I paid that punk major paper to end her life. I was sleeping with the nigga and still couldn't get him to do it. He went all sweet on me, not wanting to hit a little girl. I waved enough paper at him to change all that, though. When he got finished sniffing that cream we had a contract."

Shonda ventured close to the defense table again. She crossed her arms while staring into Tawney's tearstained, shocked, and speechless face. "Hmmph. I know you blamed it on your husband 'cause he be an O.G., right? You thought it was his street sins. It figures. You niggas that have made it out are all the same. You think you're all that."

Tawney watched her warily like a caged animal. She uttered a silent prayer under her breath to the Lord pleading with him to hear her and deliver her from the hands of this demented evil. "Jesus."

Just as she whispered the name of Jesus, Aisha, who was in her room in a suspended state between here, now, and there, wrote the name of Jesus in bold red strokes on a fresh page out of an artist sketchpad.

She slashed rather than wrote the name of the world's sacrificial lamb, Jesus Christ. The hand that wrote it trembled with a power that no child possessed.

She then ripped the page out. It fluttered in the air and she scribbled furiously again.

The baby let out a loud howl!

Tawney's heart felt like it had been ripped out as she thought about her beautiful little girl at the hands of this maniac.

She almost fainted and something inside her shut down at the thought. Somewhere in the winds of her mind a voice whispered, "Hold fast."

Shonda continued on, really starting to feel her newfound status as Superpower. "Your house got shot up and you blamed Shannon, right? Wrong. Guess who?"

She turned to stare up at the noose that was waiting for Tawney. The imagery of her hanging there swinging was already in her mind's eye. She would dispense with her, then take what was rightfully hers in the first place. "My connections reach long and far, Tawney. Sort of like yours at work."

She smiled softly, dreamily at Tawney.

"Oh, and by the way, Shannon is much better in bed than the young punks who kidnapped you. That nigga has got game, but you know that, don't you? That's why you hooked him away from the ghetto princesses. Anyway, in the end you lose. He's one of ours and he's coming back. He's gonna be treated like the fine ghetto prince that he is."

Shonda walked back behind the judge's bench. She sat down.

In contemplation she looked across at Tawney. "Spence was hot and had it going on too, but thanks to you he is no more. The last I heard he was resembling Swiss cheese somewhere."

Shonda threw the gavel at Tawney, hitting her hard right upside her head. A large egg immediately took shape on her forehead. Blood trickled down her face. The blow almost knocked her out.

Tawney struggled once again, trying to free herself. She tried to wriggle her wrists free from the tight bonds, but her fingers were pure numb. She could barely feel the binds.

She was going to choke the life out of Shonda if she got free, and she wouldn't do it quickly because she wanted to enjoy every minute of the wind exiting from her body for eternity.

Shonda continued to talk as though there hadn't been a physical interruption. "Well, you were wrong on all counts, Tawney."

Her face contorted in rage, her features squeezed together and frozen air expelled from her mouth, though how this could happen in a room in which Tawney was sweating she had no idea. "It's your corporate sins that killed your daughter, Tawney. And they're the same sins that are gonna kill you."

She came down from the bench. Closely watching her, Tawney could feel rather than see a black power trailing her. It emanated from her, shivering in the air, and it was in full control.

She rushed over, shoving the makeshift defense table hard against Tawney's chest. Tawney toppled to the floor. Shonda kicked her hard in her chest. It felt like the feet of ten men slamming into her chest. She lost air.

"Fortune rains on you, though, doesn't it Ms. Corporate? 'Cause you managed to get my man Spence. You know him, right? The one who was buried in your daughter's grave before she was even buried in it? Now, ain't that a blip?"

Shonda was seeing red. "The damn thing had her name on it and y'all flipped my boy into the dirt instead!"

She stooped down, grabbing a handful of Tawney's hair, and spat directly in her face. Tawney turned her face away.

Shonda yanked it back front and center. "You're scum, Tawney. Corporate sleazebag scum. Calling shots on people's jobs. Writing people up. Pure corporate scum, but I can tell you there are no walls from the corporate world to protect you now. Not here in this place. This is my world, Tawney. I make the laws. I break the laws. And I decide who abides by them," she stated with pure venom.

With that she kicked Tawney repeatedly in the chest. Then she stomped her in the face.

Blessedly Tawney passed out.

You are no longer an outside observer. You are now immersed in the fabric of Out A' Order.

Chapter 44

Out on the street in front of the Clinton Avenue storefront Shannon tore up to the curb. He jumped out of the car. Marcus waited until he heard the door slam shut and then he crawled out from the floor in the back of the car, on the side of the street where Shannon couldn't see him.

Shannon didn't even know he was in the car.

He also had no knowledge that this child was in such a state of fear that he had gone to the police officer Campbell for help. So had Dominique. Unbeknownst to Shannon, Campbell had been getting an earful.

Marcus was afraid Shannon was going to be killed and he couldn't stand the thought of that after having watched Jazz's blood seeping into the gutter and her mother kidnapped by thugs.

His ten-year-old mind didn't even want to think about what they had done to Jazz's mother. He shivered. Deep inside, even though he had given the address to where she was being kept, he really didn't believe she was still alive.

Those young boys who took her were feared and revered in the hood. They wreaked terror that would be written in the annals of hood law for generations to come.

Generally when they left a situation the only ones left breathing were them. They didn't leave any life in their wake. In the

Central Ward you only got one shot to make your mark. They had taken theirs.

In light of all this Marcus had talked to the cop Campbell, telling him everything because he knew that even when he whispered, "Someone please call 911," no one answered.

He didn't want to do a repeat performance, only to again relive the same nightmare. If Mrs. Davenport was dead and then they killed Jazz's daddy, that meant their whole family would have been wiped out.

The little boy just couldn't handle the thought of another call for help that would go unanswered. Little did he know that on this day it would be different, on this day the walls in the hood would come tumbling down.

He still didn't understand what he had seen the day Jazz had died, but he knew in his heart it wasn't right. Plus he hadn't told anyone that he daydreamed of that sound he'd heard on that day over and over again, and he actually heard it in his sleep as well.

It was a weird keening sound. The trees had shook, and from the corner of his eye he had thought he'd seen black wings.

Maybe not.

But if not, then why was he seeing the same exact thing in his sleep? And to add to that, somebody's baby kept crying.

He didn't know what it was, but he knew they had to fight back whatever it was because you couldn't just let somebody hit you and not hit back.

So Marcus figured it was time for the law to arrive before something happened this time instead of always after it happened. Besides he was tired of watching people dying. He had been checking out the black police officer, and he seemed like he could be trusted, so Marcus took his chances.

That Lombardo cop was a real creep and Marcus wouldn't have talked to him, even if it meant the whole block dying on the same day. In fact he had insisted that he would only talk if Campbell was alone. The black cop had obliged him.

He knew in the world he lived in, even at the age of ten, that talking to the cops was a no-no and like having your death warrant signed. But he felt like they were the living dead anyway, so what did it matter? Nobody rushed when Jazz was lying in the street dying.

He might not live through this anyway. At least he would go out stand-up and trying.

For his part, once Shannon had received the information from Marcus of where his wife was being held, tunnel vision had claimed him. At first he was shocked that Marcus had even been able to obtain the 411 on the spot.

He had to admit that little nigga had heart.

But then he decided he didn't have time to dwell on it, nor did he care as long as he knew where his wife was.

There was only one thing on his mind, and that was getting her back alive. By any means necessary. The story that Mama had shared with him, as well as the vision that had locked them together, faded from his mind as he surged forward in the power of what he knew best, the flesh.

Shannon had just stepped onto the curb when he heard his name. The sound of it was like frozen icicles. "Shannon! Freeze, nigga!" Rico's voice seared through the air like a steak sizzling on a grill.

A shot rang out.

It hit the gas tank on Shannon's car. A line of gasoline poured from it, trickling down the curb.

Marcus watched the line of gasoline from his hiding place. It trickled in slow motion, but a steady stream it was.

Papers with the name of Jesus slashed across them in red now fluttered in the air over Aisha's head as though helium were holding them up. The child's eyes were squeezed shut, and sweat was pouring from her brow. Her right hand trembled, and she kept on writing.

All she could do was write the name of Jesus. She ripped off another sheet that fluttered in the air, to join the rest of the cloud of papers already hovering there.

Mama in her house leaned her head back as her eyes rolled back up in her head. Papa and Nana Mama each sat on the side of her, not uttering a word or daring to breathe. They knew it had started. They linked hands with Mama, holding on tightly for support.

"The hand that rocks the cradle is covered in black. Take your hand off them," Mama uttered.

The baby howled.

The Darkling shrieked.

The old storefront spat bricks that rolled in the streets.

Shannon stopped in his tracks at the sound of his name. He squinted, looking down the street. He could see it had been blocked off. It was sealed off tight. It was also surrounded as though he had entered a war zone.

Like a mirage Rico appeared in front of him.

He snapped his fingers in the air. More of his crew members appeared on the roof. They appeared in the alley. They emerged from the various vehicles parked on the street.

All were strapped. They all had the lights from their Glocks trained on Shannon. Every single one of them waited with bated breath for Rico's orders. Shannon Davenport would be dead before the click of a second on a clock.

Shannon was oblivious. The blood was pounding in his temples. He had been temporarily blinded by his anger, and that was all he could see.

"I want my wife, Rico," he stated without a trace of fear.

Rico put his foot on the path toward him. Arrogantly, sarcastically, and in a voice one decibel removed from hell he said, "And I want your life, Mr. Davenport."

The two men's eyes locked into the street battle that was to come. First blood. Ballistic stepped from between the shadows of the building.

The instant Marcus saw him he shook in fear, wetting his pants. This dude was scary. He couldn't be after Mr. Davenport, because if he was there was no way he would live. Marcus knew there was little to nothing that could stop Ballistic.

What was he doing here?

Ballistic's power was such that he didn't do much more than whisper Rico's name. Yet the sound of it reverberated as a gurgle from the pavement in the streets. Seriously it was as though he had shouted it through a loudspeaker from the roof.

Rico turned to see Ballistic.

Before he could put a block on it a look of pure fear crossed his face. This dude was a living legend, and even his legend couldn't live up to him. A superior black power with no limits shivered around him, and for the first time in his life, Rico felt real fear.

Ballistic smiled knowingly.

Rico was quaking in his boots and trying hard not to show it. He knew if he did he would die, and lose for sure.

Ballistic assessed the situation, then shook his head. He had defied death more times than ten men who had already died. He had a hole in his throat to prove that he was eternal. When he left here today, not much life would be left beside him.

For the moment he would relish dealing with baby boy. He knew Rico thought he was true to da game. But he had been played because true players didn't play the game, they created it on their own terms, such as he had done.

Baby boy needed to be taught. "I told you, boy, that I would not be changing your Pampers no more."

Trey and Warren P. appeared next to Ballistic. He briefly gurgled in Trey's direction, indicating him as a favorite.

Then he returned his stare to Rico.

Shannon looked around in confusion. Something was wrong with the script. He couldn't put his finger on it, but there had been a subtle change in the air.

Suddenly he was connected to the vision. It was the same one that had happened upon him in Mama's house. He saw the girl-child Aisha scribbling furiously. Above her head floated a cloud of papers with the name of Jesus slashed across them in red.

She looked up from the pad staring straight into his eyes. In that moment he knew without a doubt that his life had somehow been spared, and he had been removed from the line of fire.

Mama prayed.

Shannon heard her clearly. "He's one of yours, Lord. Some men are chosen and some men have no choice. Do not let the blood of the sacrificial lamb pass him by. Protect him as your own. Teach him true allegiance."

In the instant that Mama spoke those words she had rebuilt a faith that had been challenged and shattered, but because of that old woman faith would be renewed, right in the hood. Right in the heart of many from whom it had been stolen.

Shannon saw a vision of a building collapse.

The old storefront building spat more bricks, directly in the street. Ballistic, Rico, and their respective crews were so locked into their street battle that they barely acknowledged the falling bricks with more than a glance.

They were caught up in flesh and ignoring the warning of the spirit.

The opposing enemies were locked in. Ballistic's hold was steady on Rico now. The totality of Ballistic's true being surged forward to connect with Rico.

For the first time Rico felt blackness in more than the flesh. He came face-to-face with a power that never deemed to lose. In an instant this young boy knew he had bitten off more than he could chew and his bowels let loose.

"You made one grave mistake, Rico. You dishonored the woman who birthed me. It is bad to dishonor a man's mother."

A look of confusion played across Rico's face. He was thrown off for a minute. "I don't know your moms, man." Silently he thought, *I didn't know the devil had a mother.*

Ballistic laughed, emitting another gurgle. He leaned heavily on his cane while advancing toward Rico and Shannon, both of whom were frozen in place.

"Of course you do, my man. You spit at her feet in the church before you broke her heart by stealing her son's body."

In that instant Rico knew for sure he was dead. But he wasn't going down without a fight. Spence Parkinson had been Ballistic's brother. That woman in the church had been his mother. This information traveled through Rico's mind like a shock wave.

His eyes widened in surprise, but he had had enough. He would never be able to regain respect within his crew because those closest to him could smell the stench of his bowels.

He had nothing to lose and everything to gain, if by some chance he pulled this off.

At that moment a shriek ripped through the air. The Darkling had arrived. The scariest thing about it was this time it wasn't loud. It made no noise and it went unnoticed, signaling the finality of things to come.

It would gather revenge and its own spoils just as it had traded for, and then it would gather for its own those who had worshipped at the wrong throne.

What was worse than that, Aisha stopped scribbling.

And Mama stopped praying.

Their world became silent as the time approached for the evil to eat its own.

The blood of the lamb would only be evoked to protect those who were right. To protect those who had the ability to step up, admitting they were wrong.

Trey, who was still standing next to Ballistic, did something he had never done before in his life as a gangster. He retreated.

There was something in the air he'd never felt before, and with it it carried great power, a power supreme. Whatever it was was not of this world.

Trey laid his weapon at Ballistic's feet. Ballistic gave him a scathing look, but this didn't alter his course of action. Sometimes you only got *one* shot.

Then he began to pray earnestly under his breath. He knew he would have to pay for all he had done, but when he met his maker his soul would be right. He wasn't going out like that.

Seeing Trey in her mind's eye, Aisha scribbled the word *Jesus*.

Mama prayed feverishly, "Take your hands off them."

Shannon Davenport heard the sound of thunder. The walls crashed all around him. It sounded like an earthquake was taking place next to his ears. The thunder was so loud it sounded like a sonic boom.

Marcus didn't even have to utter, "Someone please call 911." This time 911 was in the house for those who wanted to be right.

Rico had had as much as he was going to take. "Enough of you, nigga," he said in response to Ballistic's remark regarding his mother.

He snapped his fingers in the air.

All the weapons trained themselves on Ballistic. He was caught in the crosshairs of what amounted to a patchwork quilt of infrared lights.

A confident sarcastic smile was just about to cross Rico's lips when the script was flipped. He was a half second away from the thought *maybe I can win this. I can give the order quickly and turn this nigga into a pile of rubble and be done.*

He was almost there when Ballistic nodded.

At a nod of Ballistic's head all the weapons from Rico's crew repositioned with Rico in the eye of the storm. The crew fastened on their dead leader who was still standing, but not for long.

Ballistic had bought off Rico's entire crew and had paid dearly for it, but this was his moment and he would receive a king's ransom from that which he worshipped, or so he thought.

Rico looked around at his crew to see nothing but the faces of enemies mirrored back. The ground in the Central Ward shook on that day.

Somebody had better pray for all the wrongs. Because on this day it only shook, but all that had gone before had been recorded. A storm is one thing. A tidal wave is another.

Rico couldn't believe his eyes.

He stared at each of them. Some of these niggas had eaten in his mama's house. Yet in the final hour, there was no loyalty, no allegiance. The darkness was in place and it would eat its own.

"What the . . . ?" Rico said.

Ballistic now stepped to the curb. He blew a silent whistle. His German shepherd leaped from the alley toward Rico.

Rico could see the slobbering dog with teeth like fangs and the red demented eyes charging at him. But he was helpless to do anything about it. Before he could make a move to try to play it out so he could go down by the bullets instead, the dog was all over him.

He went straight for his throat, ripping out his windpipe and tearing him to shreds. Shannon dove under a car. Marcus ran trembling for cover at the madness taking place.

Trey got in the wind trying to put some distance between him and the insanity spewing all over the street.

Ballistic watched coldly. He was remote, and so was Warren P. as they watched the dog tear Rico apart.

The Darkling arrived in the middle of the street, her black wings now spread far and wide, preening for the world to see. She had come to claim what was hers.

Ballistic kneeled in worship, thinking he had it like that.

Warren P. backed up off the turf.

Shannon stared in fascinated fear.

Marcus now knew this was what he saw on the day Jazz died.

Amidst the dying wails of agony emitting from Rico's body the Darkling spoke.

"You have too many misses, Darryl Ross Davis," the Darkling said in its female voice, addressing Ballistic by his given name.

"Ms. Kesha got away. So did Trey." She showed him a vision of Trey on bended knee abandoning his thug persona in search of the sacrificial lamb.

The Darkling was incensed.

She had her own boss to answer to. A deal was a deal.

She had been in quite a frenzy seeing so many of the seed of her enemy gathered in one place. She had mustered as much bad feeling between them as possible, knowing they would do exactly what they had done.

Disrespect each other, suffer one another, and kill each other.

That was what they deserved for what they had done. She had traded her soul for their payment. This one in front of her she was done with.

He was just a killing machine. He knew how to kill the body, but he possessed little to no knowledge of how to destroy the soul so that it became an aftermath she could feed on and turn over to Satan.

She looked deep into Ballistic's eyes seeing the blackness of his own soul that she would reap, but he had been unable to turn all the others. He had outlived his usefulness. Contrary to his belief, he was not eternal. With that the Darkling touched the match to the gasoline that had been trickling down the curb.

It led straight to Ballistic. The fire caught the hem of his pants turning him into a flaming ball of fire. Chaos broke out and the crews began to flee the area unable to believe their eyes. They knew when it was time to get out of there.

The Darkling would become folklore that lived on in the whispers of the Central Ward, but that those not present wouldn't believe. She had just snatched the soul of Ballistic when the sound she had forever heard materialized just behind her. Only this time it wasn't a memory. It was real.

The Darkling turned.

What she saw crumbled the facade of evil that she had lived as through the years. The black wings dissipated. The clothing, the veil, the shell of him/her, all evaporated upon the sight that was before her.

"Take your hands off her," a voice whispered. The shell that had been Satan dissipated, freeing the real imprisoned woman.

Innocence graced her presence.

She ended up standing in her stocking feet as nothing but the woman she had been, before that terrible night that had locked her in with evil. Her only crime had been bearing an illegitimate child that she loved to distraction.

And so she had cursed those who had taken him from her as well as their seed. Being a mere mortal she had not known the true power of evoking evil and had therefore become imprisoned in it, as the spirit of Satan took over, wreaking havoc and stealing souls.

Freedom from this sin had not been hers until a voice whispered in all of its love, "Take your hands off her."

Before her stood Aisha Jackson, the young girl who was only eight years old. The Darkling knew who she was, for it was she who had stolen her voice, so that she couldn't speak of her.

But more than Aisha standing before her was what she held in her arms. She held the bubbling brown bouncing baby boy whom she had birthed. He stared at her with recognition in his eyes.

Aisha had found him in death and was standing with her arms outstretched, handing the child to her. Putting an end to things. She had returned him to his rightful place.

The remaining few looked on and Shannon Davenport was one of them. Marcus had come out of his hiding place and was staring at Aisha. And Trey, who hadn't gotten far, was looking from a distance on bended knee.

All the rest of them were in the wind for the time being.

The Darkling ran her hands down the flesh on her body as though she couldn't believe it. Aisha handed her the child and she took him in her arms. "Two wrongs don't make a right," Aisha said, her voice restored.

"Vengeance is mine, saith the Lord," Mama uttered.

They had just witnessed the greatest love of all even in the midst of darkness.

A tear trickled down Ms. Dorothy's face as she evaporated in the mist to face the payment for what she had done. The baby gave a last howl for the past, the present, and the future.

That one cry was enough to restore mercy for the ones who were left.

Chapter 45

"If you move I'll kill you," Shonda said as she heard a noise at the entryway. She grabbed Tawney by the scruff of her neck, putting the gun to her head. Most likely that would be some of her boys checking up on things, but you couldn't be too careful.

It was a good thing she wasn't too, because in that instant the door flew off its hinges. Shannon Davenport burst through the door. He stopped cold in his tracks upon seeing Tawney and Shonda. Shocked confusion registered on his face.

Shonda smiled at him.

Shannon hesitated.

Marcus ran through the door behind Shannon.

Tawney saw Shannon hesitate, realizing that he didn't understand the fullness of the situation. She shouted out a warning. "Shannon, don't let her fool you."

Shonda squeezed her neck tighter. "Shut up, Tawney."

Tawney coughed.

She looked at Shannon with pleading eyes. Shannon observed his battered wife, as well as the condition she was in. He dug deep for another miracle that would keep him out of the flesh, delivering his wife unto him without more bloodshed.

Back in her room now, Aisha simply showed him the paper with one name written on it. That was all it took.

Mama, Papa, and Nana Mama kept their hands linked until the final straw of this evil had been banished.

Not heeding Shonda's warning on her neck, Tawney spoke up on behalf of the dead child she had lost. "She killed Jazz, Shannon. She had our house shot up. She had me kidnapped. She slept with you to get back at me."

Shannon flinched on the last sentence, but truth was truth and now was not the time to dwell on it. He had to get his wife back without further damage.

Shonda flung Tawney to the floor.

She trained the Uzi on her. Momentarily she glanced at the noose hanging from the ceiling, regretting there wouldn't be time now to hang Tawney from it, unless, well, unless maybe she steered Shannon over to her side.

Shannon followed her line of vision. When he saw the noose and read her thoughts it was all he could do to keep from killing this woman.

She killed his daughter and now she was thinking about hanging his wife. She was insane.

Shonda looked coyly at Shannon. Sweet as honey she said, "She's lying."

Shannon moved closer to her. She turned the gun on him.

Then she remembered she needed to keep Tawney covered. She turned the gun back to her. She wavered between the two of them. Damn, she wished she had two guns, one for each hand, and one for each of them, in case Shannon didn't comply.

Oh well. One would have to do under the circumstances. She decided to cover Tawney.

"Put the gun down, Shonda," Shannon requested.

Shonda looked him up and down, remembering, then decided she'd better keep her focus. "I'm sorry, I can't do that. She's a sellout, man. You don't need her. You've got me."

Shannon searched the depths of the insanity standing before him. He probed its recesses. "Did you kill my daughter, Shonda?"

Shonda wiped the sweat from her brow with one hand, while keeping the gun focused on Tawney with the other. She laughed nervously. It sounded like Shannon might be a little mad at her, but she'd fix that as soon as she got rid of Tawney.

"Naw, baby, it ain't like that. I didn't. I killed Tawney's daughter, not yours. But it's okay because we can make more."

Shannon would have closed his eyes at the pain of her words, but that definitely couldn't happen.

In a singsongy voice Shonda mimicked Tawney. "Jazz did this and Jazz did that. Jazz did this and Jazz did that." Her eyes glazed over. Foam now bubbled from the side of her mouth.

"You and I can be together without her in the way. I'll be making as much money as Tawney. I'm going to have her job now."

Shonda tired of the charade. She had the gun trained on Tawney. She squeezed the trigger.

Shannon shouted, "Shonda, no!"

Marcus came out of his shock. He ran unthinkingly over to Shonda. He dove for her legs and bit her. The shot rang out in the air, removing Tawney from the focus of the weapon as Shonda shrieked from the pain of being bitten.

"You're out a' order," Marcus shouted with tears in his eyes.

Crazed from his bite Shonda repositioned the gun, training it on Marcus.

Shannon dove on top of her.

A black hand rocked the cradle in their midst.

It was only an illusion. They say the hand that rocks the cradle rules the world, in this case the evil was no longer rocking.

Just as the shot was released Mama prayed in the spirit once again, "Take your hands off them."

Tears ran in a stream from her eyes.

"He says you can't have them. Take your hands off our children, you beast." The black hand disappeared from the cradle.

Then there was calm.

Papa, Mama, and Nana Mama all cried as they felt the tentacles of evil slip away as they tried to save the last child in association with this particular madness.

The fight went out of Shonda as the last words were uttered. The final door to her mind slammed shut. The Uzi clattered to the floor.

All of them lay sprawled on the floor. Shannon crawled over to Tawney, kicking the Uzi as far away as possible. He didn't even want to touch it with his hands.

He held Tawney in his arms. Marcus looked at him. He beckoned him over for a hug. The little boy had been through a lot. Marcus sat squeezed in between Shannon and Tawney in a circle of love.

Shonda sat up looking at them and what she would never have. All the fight had been knocked out of her. And in that instant her mind went totally blank. There would be no recall.

She gazed around as if she didn't know where she was or what had happened. There was nothing but a vacancy reflected from her eyes.

Campbell and Lombardo came through the door Shannon had crashed through. They assessed the situation.

Lombardo took a look at Shannon and a silent understanding passed between them. He gave a nod of respect to Shannon before placing Shonda in handcuffs and under arrest.

Campbell smiled offering Shannon his hand to pull him and his family up off the floor. Well, Marcus wasn't his son but he sure was family.

At her house Aisha leaned over her mother, who was sleeping on the couch. "Hi, Mommy," she whispered, kissing her on the cheek. Nikki sat up in shock. She would never know the full story of what her daughter had suffered or why she had lost her voice.

In the course of things it really didn't matter.

Aisha had been an instrument in the fight to regain good.

Trey would later confess to the crimes of his gang life. The one that scarred his heart the most was Kesha's murder. He only confessed to his own participation. He wouldn't take anyone else down with him.

He decided he'd rather face his wrongs and pay in the flesh than reap a payment he knew he couldn't pay in the spirit.

From what he had witnessed he believed that while you were here you still had time. In this way when the time came he'd have a clean start.

There was just no way he was going out like that. His hands

were not clean, he knew for that he needed to pay. That's why he was doing his time. But he was on bended knee that yet he might live.

And he sat on the cold, hard cement floor of his cell in a prayer of forgiveness every single night.

For his part Shannon Davenport would never forget what he had seen and how he had witnessed a power that had assured him that with one child and a pen he could surely win. That he could stop the river of blood from flowing.

Simply by his belief.

The walls had come tumbling down. Just like the Jericho wall, such were the walls in the hood. The misdeeds and evil were passing through the generations.

It needed to stop.

That was why he had gone into the storefront unarmed. He had decided to trust Jesus. And with that his faith that had at one time been challenged, as well as shattered, had been rebuilt and was now renewed.

Papa, Mama, and Nana Mama finally unlinked hands, knowing that all had been fulfilled for the time being.

Mama only wondered what would have happened long ago if she had uttered the words on the night of Ms. Dorothy's death. "Take your hands off them, you beast. Take your *hands* off them."

You have been reading Out "A" Order.

We need to be mindful of the hand that rocks the cradle. I wish I could say that "you are at the end of the story" but alas, it is not so. I know you know that. All you've got to do is look around.

I did forewarn you that you would need to see with your spirit, not just with your eyes. I told you that upon this reading you had deemed to enter a different world.

I made it clear that it was a world that coexisted by its own laws. And that that world was in and of itself OUT A' ORDER!

Usually I type the words "The End" when I'm finished with a story. I can't even do that with Out "A" Order. I tried but I had to delete it.

I'll let you figure out when it's over.

A READING GROUP GUIDE

OUT "A" ORDER

EVIE RHODES

ABOUT THIS GUIDE

The suggested questions are intended to enhance your group's reading of this book.

DISCUSSION QUESTIONS

1. Why is Shannon Davenport suspect in his daughter's death?

2. Was Tawney Davenport right in blaming Shannon for their daughter's death or was her grief misplaced?

3. Who shot Jasmine Davenport? Why?

4. Does the model city of Newark, New Jersey used in this book reflect other cities in the country? And if so in what ways?

5. What is the underlying message in *Out "A" Order*?

6. What is the first person narration voice reflective of throughout?

7. Why do you think Shonda Hunt's behavior was so masked? And why did people miss the warning signs?

8. What do you think life would be like if people were able to be both judge and jury over people whom they think have wronged them?

9. In addition to Jazz's death, what was the other thing that hurt Marcus with regard to her passing?

10. What are some of the circumstances that create persons such as Ballistic?

11. What was the unpardonable sin committed by Rico De-Leon Hudson.

12. What was the single event that led to Ms. Dorothy's repentance?

13. Who or what restored Aisha's speech?

14. Why did Mama utter the words "Take your hands off our children you beast! Take your hands off them!" And what does she mean?

GREAT BOOKS, GREAT SAVINGS!

When You Visit Our Website:
www.kensingtonbooks.com

You Can Save Money Off The Retail Price
Of Any Book You Purchase!

- All Your Favorite Kensington Authors
- New Releases & Timeless Classics
- Overnight Shipping Available
- eBooks Available For Many Titles
- All Major Credit Cards Accepted

Visit Us Today To Start Saving!
www.kensingtonbooks.com

All Orders Are Subject To Availability.
Shipping and Handling Charges Apply.
Offers and Prices Subject To Change Without Notice